PARIKRAMA

Stories

by

Radhika Vyas Sharma

FROG BOOKS

ISBN 978-93-52017-25-6
Copyright © Radhika Vyas Sharma, 2016

First published in India 2016 by Frog Books
An imprint of Leadstart Publishing Pvt Ltd
1 Level, Trade Centre
Bandra Kurla Complex
Bandra (East) Mumbai 400 051 India
Telephone: +91-22-40700804
Fax: +91-22-40700800
Email: info@leadstartcorp.com
www.leadstartcorp.com / www.frogbooks.net

Sales Office:
Unit No.25, Building No.A/1,
Near Wadala RTO,
Wadala (East), Mumbai – 400037 India
Phone: +91 22 24046887

US Office:
Axis Corp, 7845 E Oakbrook Circle
Madison, WI 53717 USA

Editor: Tanzeel Saiyed
Cover: Shynu Koshy
Layouts: Chandravadan Ramchandra Shiroorkar

Typeset in Palatino Linotype & Verdana
Printed at Repro

For my Father, Papaji.

An exemplary admirer of the harmony of language.

About the Author

Radhika Vyas Sharma has been writing for over fifteen years and is currently at work on a novel. Radhika received her MFA in Creative Writing from the SF State University; notable honors include a teaching assistantship at San Francisco State University, and a semester as Assistant Fiction Editor at 14 Hills: SF State's Graudate Literary Journal. Postgraduate work includes VONA: Voices of our Nation Foundation Workshops at UC Berkeley and Vermont Post Graduate Writer's Conference. Radhika's writing credits include reviews and features for The San Francisco Chronicle, The San Jose Mercury News, The Times of India, The Economic Times, KQED FM's Forum, Pacific Time and Perspectives, India Currents and several others. A short story *Daddy Cool* was featured in The Santa Clara Review, Spring 2010. Another story, *Just a Photograph* was showcased by Kearny Street Workshop in APAture 2013: Window into the work of Emerging Asian Pacific Artists.

Contents

A Note from the Author.

Many of the stories in this collection started as fragmented vignettes on the page in the early 2000's while a few others came to me fully-formed, simply requiring transcription on the page. A brief stint as a features journalist for many Diaspora publications in the San Francisco Bay Area informed these incubating stories as did the aspiration of so many young immigrants I saw around me. And while the technologies of communication have changed dramatically in the past decade and half – long gone are the days of EMS post delivered letters and the collect call – what has endured is the need to stay connected to the motherland even as the pressures of day- to-day living rapidly shift the immigrant's allegiances.

It will forever remain a mystery why people leave their homes. The usual answers are: for better livelihood, better standards of work and life but for the most part they are all just answers that ring true only in that moment. Even as the politics of economics remains a consistent backdrop to these stories, these stories are really just about people; men, women and children dealing with the challenges of living, losing and loving. It is my hope that each reader will find a slice of themselves in at-least one of the sentences in this book's pages. It is a benediction when a story reaches out to us to be read or written; for the world wants us to be lonely and stories remind us that we are not alone.

-Radhika Vyas Sharma.

Beneath Her Veil the Stars Faded Away

Saru Chachi was the neighborhood's favorite subject of discussion. Depending upon the drift in the air, she was either vilified as an abrupt, self-absorbed sleeveless blousewearing harridan or hailed as the emancipated woman ahead of her times.

But no matter what anyone said, Rajshri liked Saru Chachi; Rajshri's four meetings with Saru Chachi had been enough to make up her mind. Rajshri's mother-in-law, Taru Ma, liked Saru Chachi as well. Saru Chachi had already been invited twice for tea, an invitation she declined both times, pleading work at the adult school she presided over in the capacity of vice-principal. But beetel nut chewing Taru Ma, daughter (and now sister) of the most famous sweet maker in town was nothing if not persistent. Finally, Saru Chachi relented and came visiting one Friday evening, right at the end of her school week. While Rajshri stood next to the gas stove in the perpetually damp and dim lit kitchen, adjusting the loose end of her sari snugly on her hair, her gaze alternating between the overloaded food tray kept on the kitchen countertop (stocked with vegetable cutlets, sweet chick pea orbs *ladoos*, four porcelain cup plates and an empty tea pot) and the open mouthed cooking utensil bubbling with strong ginger chai, Taru Ma sat next to Saru Chachi in the drawing room on the blue block-print covered divan, fingering her Barmeri shawl and said,"What Saru *behen,* you've started acting like the big city people nowadays, using the "always busy" card and refuse to meet us. You must visit us more, chat, watch TV serials with us. We were in school together remember? I remember how everyone confused us to be sisters; being of the same complexion, height, and of course, our names rhyme as well!"

"I'm not sure I recollect Taruna," said Saru Chachi, "But you must forgive me, that was forty five years ago and plus you barely stayed in school till class four."

Taru Ma coughed a forced cough and glared first at that mole on Saru Chachi's cheek and then at the crisp saffron *Kota* cotton sari Saru Chachi was wearing. While God had cursed Saru Chachi with three miscarriages and subsequent infertility, he had made up for it by taking her mother-in-law within a decade of her marriage and by supplying her with a mild-mannered businessman for a husband who brought her delectable saris from his travels.

"*Haan haan*, I am not as lucky as you are, born to a father who let you go to high school and then married to a husband who let you do B.A and B Ed. What to do? I am only a simple woman who *only* knows how to cook and scrub and cook some more. I only know how to take care of my home *and* children..." said Taru Ma, a distant tone creeping in her voice. From the kitchen door Rajshri caught a hint of darkness sweep across Saru Chachi's face but Taru Ma went on, "Children, they are such a pleasure…." At this, Rajshri turned off the gas stove, picked up the food tray and decided to walk towards the drawing room, even though the tea was not quite ready and would now need to be poured and served in another round.

The faint *Chum Chum* jingling of Rajshri's anklets announced the arrival of food. As Rajshri put the food tray on the rickety jute table with wooden legs set in front of the two older women, Saru Chachi's eyes widened with mild astonishment as she observed the carefully guarded bump on Rajshri's slim frame, something that had escaped her notice earlier.

"I didn't know you were going to have a little one in your home soon, Taruna," she said to Taru Ma and then to Rajshri, "May God bless you *beta*." Rajshri nodded from under her *ghunghat*, her diaphanous veil, and touched Saru Chachi's feet before setting out in the direction of the kitchen again.

"See, that's what I meant when I said you should visit us more often. Yes, yes, a little one is to play in our house again, in four months," Taru Ma laughed her raspy half-throaty laugh, "But this time, I will be a different kind of grandmother. This time I will become a *dadi*, a child from my son, this one, and this little one will not fly away like the one I nursed for three months two summer's ago, my daughter's infant." Then as Rajshri was waddling back into the kitchen, she heard her mother-in-law finally hit it, "Saru, you *chupi rustom*, you didn't even tell me that your sister-in-law's son lives in *Amrica?* What a lucky woman your sister-in-law must be to have a son who sends her all those imported shampoos and creams, *haan!*" Saru Chachi nodded, pretending not to catch on.

"How is Bhimsen *Bhai Saab* doing? And I didn't see Ramesh around, looks like he finally got a job?" asked Saru Chachi to change the topic but Taru Ma was an old hand at this. "Haan*, Haan*, Suman's father is busy with his work at the magistrate's office, works very hard. He will soon have to put in overtime now that our little Suman is of marriageable age. And with your nephew being of marriageable age too, *aarre* look there, Suman's back from college, I can hear her scooty near the door."

Suman walked in wearing her latest salwar kameez, mauve drawstring pants paired with a collared saffron zari tunic, a tacky imitation of the latest Hindi film fashion and immediately blushed at the sight of Saru Chachi sitting uncomfortably on the bed sheet that she'd embroidered over the summer. "Arre, beta, see Saru Chachi is here to help you become the princess you already are. You must be so hungry, bas, beta, food is almost ready. Rajshri!" Taru Ma, an old hand at this type of communication only just turned her face slightly towards the cold and tiny kitchen. But Rajshri did not answer with her mousy "yes Taru Ma" this time; she responded with the disconcerting sounds of her retching in the bathroom across the kitchen.

"Rajshri is not feeling too well, Taruna," said Saru Chachi, getting up from the divan. "*Arre*, Saru all that is normal when women are pregnant," dismissed Taru Ma with a careless wave of her hand, "Come come, let us not disturb her. I've heard that your nephew is well settled in Amrica now and that your sister in law is looking for brides and ... and so tell me, do you think my little Suman will appeal to your sister-in-law?"

Saru Chachi sat down on the divan pensively, then after what seemed an eternity to Taru Ma she opened her mouth and said, "*Bahut, Bahut* - Very much, very much."

*

Taruna had always been Rajshri's Taru Ma, for Taruna had claimed Rajshri for her only son the moment she was born.

"Why have her call me something else when she will have to call me Ma sooner or later," she had said triumphantly to her erstwhile neighbor Sulekha. Therefore, Rajshri called Taruna, Taru Ma, from the moment her learnt cognition and speech and waited for the day her time with this adopted mother would supercede that with her biological mother. And within no time she was there. There were many new things about marriage for Rajshri. The new orange, pink and vermillion saris, the *kundan* etched gold sets, the rich food that was forced down her throat and the *ghunghat,* the veil, which had now enlisted her in its ranks as well. But the biggest change was the malevolent shine Rajshri saw in Taru Ma's eyes and the reflexive tightening in her chest that Rajshri experienced, whenever she encountered *that* look.

Rajshri did not have too many memories of Taru Ma as a child, but on the few occasions that she'd met her future mother-in-law before marriage Taru Ma had seemed nice enough. A little edgy but still nice. Of course, all that was gone now.

One morning, in her first week as a new bride, Rajshri woke up at 8 am and was welcomed by an eerie silence as she hurried to assist Taru Ma with the household activities. "Rajshri, things are not the same anymore," Taru Ma said ominously before wiping the sweat from her brow with her *pallu,* the loose end of her sun bleached polyester sari. Three miscarriages. Two daughters. One son. Countless hours of standing in front of smoky ovens. Taru Ma had endured enough. Now it was time to pass it on. Gone were the occasional days when Rajshri could wake up at 9 a.m., saunter in her mother's kitchen and be the first to eat breakfast in her family. Marriage had birthed a new Rajshri by mutation, a Rajshri who would put the welfare of all others above hers. While overall Rajshri had been trained for this, it still felt unreal. Somehow her days at school had given her hope that she would escape this sudden shame, this forced show of respect. This spontaneous pulling of the veil as soon as she came face to face with any man. This transformation of the *ghunghat* into a hijab-like apparition in front of other women, boldly stopping at the contours of the forehead. But like so many others before her, Rajshri had been wrong.

"So many years of *seva,* of assisting, of loving, and now what do I get from the younger generation?"

Taru Ma asked this rhetorical question many times during the day, while Rajshri cleaned, scrubbed, served tea, pakoras, *mathari* and halwa. This she did wearing gaudy dark reds, mauves and oranges, even though the ferocity of those colours made her head ache. Then one day it dawned on Rajshri that no matter how many cups of tea she prepared, or the number of cabinets she cleaned, her love would always be held up for examination, until she delivered what was expected of her.

"What a nice *bahu* you have, Taru," the women in the locality would say.

"Docile like a cow," added the hard to please Savitri Aunty.

"But what good is a cow that does not give milk?" said Taru Ma dejectedly.

At this the women would look at each other and nod their heads in agreement.

It was not as if Taru Ma had not tried. The only respectable bedroom (with one door and one window) in their three room home was given to Ramesh and Rajshri each night for the purposes of nightly consummation. The subsequent morning Taru Ma's eyes would follow Rajshri's slim frame with the relentless vigil of a soldier on the border, almost as if every night held within itself the potential to sprout another seed of her family tree. One morning Rajshri threw up and Taruna promptly called her neighborhood mid-wife to come and check Rajshri's pulse. "Oh, she's well Taru, just some indigestion," said the amused, toothless old woman. "She's always well *Mai*, always well, never anything else," replied Taru Ma despondently.

Therefore, a quarter year later, Rajshri was ecstatic when she felt the sudden urge to throw away the *gobi mutter* and yellow rice that had been put on her plate for lunch. But this was news that must be first shared with someone who loved her. Some one who had done more than grudgingly accept her presence. This good news must be first shared with mother. But today was only Tuesday; Sunday was still many days away. Nevertheless, Rajshri sneaked out that afternoon to the nearest Public Call Office, when everyone was napping, and told her mother, Sulekha. It would be two decades before India would awake to the ubiquitous cell phone. For now, it was enough to be so placid that one year be indistinguishable from another. For now, the yellow STD booth would suffice as the messenger.

"Thank benevolent Krishna! May He be praised! Now let's hope it's a boy," said Sulekha, more relieved than ecstatic. Rajshri was stunned. She had hoped that the baby would do a little something to add color to her life, to elevate her status in the family and placate Taru Ma. But now she realized that just about any baby would not do. It had to be a particular kind of baby.

Ramesh laughed when she confided in him, " Why do you worry? It will be a boy!" he said frothing with the confidence of his new found job. "But what if its not?" asked Rajshri. "Let's ask the stars tonight," winked Ramesh.

The nights were their escape, the only time Rajshri felt like she possessed Ramesh, her marriage, or even her life. One night, soon after they were married, Ramesh and Rajshri tiptoed around the house seeking refuge on the terrace, exhausted by the omnipresent voices that hardly ever allowed them a shred of privacy. That first night on the terrace had been magical. Rajshri gazed at the stars, greedily taking in lungfuls of oxygen, while Ramesh would empty his pockets filled with Rajshri's gift; fragrant *mogra* flowers bought on his way back from work, from child hawkers swarming outside the neighborhood Shiv temple. Such nights Rajshri would cry a little, her head on Ramesh's shoulders, as Ramesh caressed her fingers. But in the morning, they would become strangers again, their only touch, their only connection being through the food served and consumed. These nightly meetings had become sporadic since the time the baby had set up residence in Rajshri's womb, and even though Ramesh and Rajshri both missed their nightly excursions, its elimination had become inevitable. Rajshri had little energy left after a day filled with regular activities, and on the few occasions Ramesh nudged her, she'd bury her face in a pillow and continue sleeping.

*

In the month that followed Saru Chachi coming for chai, lunch, chai again, and also for a rare dinner with her husband, Arvind Chacha, dinner time afforded Bhimsen and Ramesh the opportunity to add some ammunition to the rounds that Taru Ma had been valiantly firing on her own.

During each visit Saru Chachi would bring something for Rajshri – usually a food festish favored by expectant mothers. Initially Saru Chachi would put the food item out on the small wooden table near the divan, but once after she saw Suman help herself to three of the four pieces of *rasgullas* she had brought for Rajshri, Saru Chachi kept things in her enormous purse, sneaking them to Rajshri during private moments. On her part, Rajshri would make an extra effort of ignore whatever bodily discomfort she was experiencing and wait for Saru Chachi with the strongest cup of chai she could decoct. After enduring months of sustained neglect, Saru Chachi's simple gestures appeared extraordinary. It pleased her to see this awkward, new camaraderie and thawing of relations between Saru Chachi and Taru Ma; but Taru Ma being Taru Ma often lapsed into her old ways, violently criticizing Saru Chachi behind her back. Once when Rajshri could take it no more, she interjected and tried to deflect the conversation, "Taru Ma, my mother has enquired what colour sari she should bring for you when she comes to take me home for delivery?"

"What does it matter? She never gets the colour right," said Taru Ma adding, "Keep mum about the date of the function in front of Saru, I don't want her inauspicious presence to mar it!"

A few weeks later (after being needled by Taru Ma and Bhimsen at the previous dinner), Saru Chachi brought photos of her nephew and his fabulous house in Chicago. Taru Ma's mind was immediately flooded by a vision of Suman alighting from an airplane, wearing tight slacks and cropped tunic paired with the oversized dark glasses that heroines of her hey-day used to favor. Or maybe Suman would favor the sleek sleeveless chiffon summer dresses and over-sized hand bags that today's film stars seemed to prefer. But whatever the result, Suman looked ravishing, unlike Taru Ma had ever been afforded the opportunity to look.

"Oh Saru you must get us an audience with your sister-in-law soon!" squealed Taru Ma when she saw Saru Chachi's nephew's tanned visage juxtaposed against the background of a three bedroom, two and a half-bath home in a Illinois suburb.

"Yes, yes. Soon," muttered Saru Chachi.

The following week, Saru Chachi arrived early and uninvited one morning, with a strong sense of urgency.

"Taru, you must help me. One of my assistants at school has suddenly taken ill, and I need help with the upcoming Republic Day celebration preparations. I was wondering if I could take Rajshri to assist me for the day?"

Taru Ma knit and purled her brows together. Rajshri stopped kneading the dough for the chapattis and crouched a little more on the wooden stool she was sitting on, her ears perked under her pink *ghunghat*. Taru Ma wiped a bit of the perspiration from her forehead from the loose end of her sari and gulped, "I need help with the cooking and besides Rajshri leaves for her mother's house in three days and she has lots of packing to do," Taru Ma wavered, "Why not take Suman?" she offered.

"Oh no, Suman will have to miss college and I will not allow that during this crucial pre-exam season. Also, my sister-in-law is going to be in town next week and ..."

"*Haan, Haan*, its fine then. All settled," Taru Ma jumped in; parting her lips to expose her beetle nut stained teeth and hoping that the act would pass for a smile. Till Suman had safely made her way across the seas Taru Ma needed Saru Chachi to be kept in good humor.

Situation resolved, an auto rickshaw was called for and Saru Chachi and Rajshri bundled in it. Ramesh escorted the rickshaw outside the gully on his TVS Honda Scooter and waved Rajshri an exuberant goodbye. "Saru Chachi, I am not sure how much I can be of help," said Rajshri inside the auto, turning to face Saru Chachi as soon as Ramesh was out of sight.

"There's not much to do. I am sure it'll come easily," said Saru Chachi confidently. The rickshaw clattered on the uneven road and fearlessly made its way through the narrow gully carved between parallel rows of brightly plastered concrete houses; houses that shared walls, history and secrets; houses which suffocated each other with their interminable gaze. Soon it was on a wider road filled with heterogeneous traffic. As they passed Saru Chachi's adult school, Rajshri jumped a little in her seat, "Where are we going Saru Chachi? This auto driver has left the school behind!" said Rajshri.

In response Saru Chachi asked, "What do you like eat nowadays, beta?"

Rajshri looked at her incredulously and then said "*Pani puri,*" a little shyly.

"I thought so," said Saru Chachi.

It was a good time to be exploring the fair grounds, the *maidan,* as it was still not as dusty as it would be later during the day. Plus, there were not as many women to jostle with in the fair either; they would start trickling-in in the afternoon, after all the household chores were done. As they paid off the auto rickshaw driver Saru Chachi said to Rajshri, "If you want you can wear your sari easily, beta. I don't think anyone will know us here." Still Rajshri did not loosen her grip on her *pallu* and still kept one end of it tucked behind her ears. The vendors were all geared up, even though their audience was running late. Smiling teenagers gifted them a *gainda* flower each and as Saru Chachi and Rajshri sauntered inside the fair grounds, they saw stalls stocked with the bright hued batik tie and dye sheets, bangle sellers, fruit juice stalls, ceramic housewares, mehndi artists, and next door, a modest play area populated with two small merry go rounds and a giant Ferris wheel. "First, let's go and try some bangles," said Saru Chachi.

The bangle seller was eager to please these two ladies, his first customers, for it was his time of *boauni,* the first transaction, which would set the tone for the business for work day. They tried on many kinds of bangles - glass, lac, plastic, metal and each in their favorite shades, burgundy, rose, teal and saffron. Rajshri tried on the bangles hesitantly, frequently glancing over her shoulder, but soon Saru Chachi's enthusiasm infected her as well. As they debated excitedly on the colours and bargained vigorously with the bangle seller, Rajshri and Saru Chachi both seemed transfixed by the thought of possessing a few colorful, fragile glass bangles; neither did Saru Chachi look the stern school Vice-Principal, nor were Rajshri's shoulders drooping as much. Eventually Rajshri chose a modestly priced set of two dozen polka-dotted burgundy glass bangles, while Saru Chachi bought two large saffron bracelets made of shellac and a lavish set of red-gold bangles. As the vendor busied himself packing the bangles in old Hindi newsprint and subsequently tying the packages with thick cotton thread, Rajshri observed, "He's given us two sizes small in the reds Saru Chachi."

"That's alright Rajshri, I asked him to - it's a gift for someone," said Saru Chachi.

Saru Chachi paid for the both of them and then slipped the of box sepia-red bangles inside Rajshri's purse.

"Oh Saru Chachi," sighed Rajshri softly.

"Now how about some *pani puri*?" asked Saru Chachi.

The mint chutney was a little sharp and the tamarind was way too sweet. Saru Chachi stopped after one plate, but Rajshri loved this crazy combination wolfing down three plates of brown crispy *puris* filled with potatoes, moong dal sprouts dunked in a heady watery concoction of chutney's, and spices. With the last of the *puris* stuffed in her mouth, Rajshri squealed so loudly that she startled Saru Chachi.

"Oh Saru Chachi! Look at that - lets go on the ferris wheel!"

"*Beta,* you are in your seventh month!"

"Don't worry Saru Chachi, this ferris wheel is one of the slower ones. I am going to be fine, I know myself," pleaded Rajshri.

"I am not so sure," replied Saru Chachi.

"Oh please, it's been almost three years since I've been on one – so long. Please, please," said Rajshri.

After ten minutes of coaxing, Saru Chachi gave in. It took another 15 minutes and a lie ("only five months old baby") to convince the ferris wheel operator. It was past noon when the wobbly ferris wheel took off. Even though the desert sun was now out, the air was crisp with January freshness and inadvertently Rajshri let her *pallu* slip so that it was not covering her head anymore. The ferris wheel took one circle, then another. Saru Chachi holding on to Rajshri in a firm grip, Rajshri laughing, feeling the air on her face, her skin feeling like she used to, before her face became her shame, the wideness of her thin lips crinkling the folds of the skin near her eyes. The giddiness of height was prolonged by the operator's decision to suspend the wheel in mid air for a few seconds. In those brief moments of suspension, Rajshri and Saru Chachi's partly-hunched bodies looked mesmerized at the landscape that's been their home and that of their mothers and grandmothers. Inexplicably, denuded desert mountains which often faded in the backdrop now appeared majestic and almost welcoming.

"You noticed my gaze linger at the flyer about the fair in Suman's hand last time didn't you, Saru Chachi?" said Rajshri

Saru Chachi nodded.

The ferris wheel moved a little and was now at its highest point of elevation.

"Taru Ma doesn't like you too much Saru Chachi...." said Rajshri.

"None of them do; it doesn't matter anymore, my dear," said Saru Chachi.

As the ferris wheel began its descent, Rajshri asked Saru Chachi, "Saru Chachi, can anyone be happy in secret?"

Saru Chachi did not take her eyes off the fair and its stalls and replied, "What do you think happens in a mother's womb Rajshri?"

A few minutes later as they finished the final dregs of their lassi, their sweaty hands fumbling with their purchases and the tall lassi glasses, Saru Chachi said with some urgency, "Lets wind up here. It's getting close to noon and I want to take you to meet a good friend of mine before I drop you back home, Rajshri."

*

The doctor's clinic was a single 10 X 8 feet room separated from her assistant's booth by a curtain made of an old bedsheet. The walls were musty beige, their mustiness barely offset by the faded calendars of smiling chubby babies.

"So Saru, how are you? And who is this young lady?" asked Dr. Sharada Batra.

"A very special little girl," said Saru Chachi with a smile, "Will you check her up for me?"

"Of course, would you like to get a sonogram as well?" asked Dr. Batra.

Saru Chachi opened her mouth to say something but Rajshri answered simply, "Yes. We'd like that very much," and then whispered to Saru Chachi, "I learnt in school what a sonogram can do."

As the assistant wheeled in the worn out computer monitor and plugged it in, Rajshri felt the kicks of her baby stronger than she had ever felt them in her 7 months as an expectant mother. The coolness of the gel Dr. Batra applied on her belly combined with the anxiety of being away from home for so long, now made her shiver.

"Take a deep breath," said Dr. Batra.

Rajshri laid with her head raised upright, her eyes fixed on the monitor, unable to relax.

"First time sonogram?" asked Dr. Batra not particularly incredulously.

"Yes, Madhvi Dai is taking care of her," replied Saru Chachi.

Dr. Batra switched on the monitor and adjusted the probe on Rajshri's belly – a few seconds later, almost miraculously, they saw the image of baby on the computer screen. In pin-drop silence, the three women watched in awe as the baby's teeny-weeny fingers made a fist and then rubbed its eyes and yawned, perhaps startled by this intrusion.

"*Kya aap hum ko to aapp bata sakte hai*? Can you tell us…?" asked Saru Chachi.

"*Ladki hai!* It's a girl," said the lady doctor wearily and switched on the dim light in the clinic to allow Rajshri to properly tie back her drawstring petticoat and adjust her sari.

This new revelation had a quietening effect on both Saru Chachi and Rajshri. Saru Chachi pulled out an envelope from her purse and kept it in front of Dr. Batra.

"*Nahin,* Saru. Not from you," said Dr. Batra and pushed the envelope away. Saru Chachi smiled. Dr. Batra was the closest she had to a friend who was her equal in intellect and life circumstance. Saru Chachi made mental note to do something special for Dr. Batra in lieu of the envelope of cash that had been returned to her. The clock struck five and the sun was ready to set. Rajshri stood up from the examination table, suddenly alert and afraid. "Shall we go home now?"

On the auto ride back home Rajshri asked, "Why all this for me Saru Chachi?"

"Think of it as birthday gift. I saw the card near the study table on my last visit. You will be 22 tomorrow. May you have a long and prosperous life!" Saru Chachi said, her voice quivering with emotion. Tears dribbled from Rajshri's eyes into her lap after bouncing off her chin and belly.

"What if the happiness wants to spill over to the rest of your life, Saru Chachi?"

"Hold on my dear, just another week and then you'll be able to enjoy your mother's company for many months. Unlike the *ghunghat,* a practice that has outlived its utility, the practice of sending girls to their mother's home for delivery is still useful," said Saru Chachi fighting back the lump in her throat.

*

As the auto rickshaw snaked its way inside the narrow *gulli*, undeterred by the overhanging mire of cable, telephone and electric wires, the parallel gutters overflowing with a curious mixture of milk, muddy water and refuse flanking it or the pedestrians forced to seek refuge on strangers' doorsteps to avoid being run over by the auto, Rajshri thought about her unborn daughter. Would her unborn too stand in a stranger's kitchen and feel unloved for the rest of her life? Would she too retch and vomit in secret corners with no one to massage her back or press her feet? As the auto got closer to its destination Rajshri felt flooded by a wave of fear and apprehension. Suddenly, she found herself wishing for a minor catastrophe like an auto failure, and that she might have never met Taru Ma.

"Saru, you thieving snake of a woman!" Taru Ma screamed as soon as the auto rickshaw stopped beside its destination. Bhimsen, Suman, Taru Ma, Savitri Aunty; the entire household seemed to have been holding their breath for the two women.

"What's the matter Taruna," said Saru Chachi quietly as she dipped into her purse to find change to dispose off the auto driver.

"Of course, nothing is the matter. You whisk my pregnant daughter-in-law to a fair and nothing is the matter. Your sister-in-law's son is already being spoken for to some big city girl and of course, nothing is the matter."

"Oh, so you know."

"Yes!" Taru Ma hissed.

"Rajshri did not ask to go to the fair. I took her there, it was my birthday gift to her," replied Saru Chachi.

"Who are you to go around giving birthday gifts to my daughter-in-law? Don't you have enough people to fool in that center of yours?" asked Taru Ma, her voice rising and moving two steps closer to Saru Chachi.

"Taruna, you certainly have very changed manners today!" said Saru Chachi stepping back. "Well, I am a simple woman. But sometimes I have to learn from conniving people like you, Saru. What do you say Suman?" Suman bobbed her fancily coiffured head, her lips zippered tight. Then Taru Ma turned her attention towards Rajshri.

"Tell her, tell her, this will not do...tell her I say," Taru Ma tugged at Bhimsen's kurta. "Taruna control yourself, the girl is expecting," said Saru Chachi.

"You childless bitch! Barren *banj*, stay away from my house!" Taru Ma's words ricocheted through the air like a guided missile sucking the air out of its surroundings. Saru Chachi was stunned. Her oversized black purse and shawl slipped from her shoulders, and as she stood facing Taru Ma, her face crumpled like the lilac lace handkerchief Rajshri was holding in her hand. Very quietly, Saru Chachi picked up her belongings, the bag of full of purchases, and turned to go. The screaming brought Ramesh outside; he joined the half-paralyzed Savitri Aunty near the door with his wet hands, having gotten up mid-meal. "Wait, Saru Chachi!" It was Rajshri, her face pale, her voice weak, her knees shaking. The baby had stopped kicking. This happened often and mostly when Rajshri was under duress. Saru Chachi turned, Rajshri ran to hug her awkwardly. Then facing Taru Ma she said, "It is a good thing God did not give you any children, because people who have them don't seem to know what to do with them." Everyone fell quiet, shocked at Rajshri's speaking out of turn. No one was more surprised than Rajshri herself. "It's a good thing that God has not restricted your focus to a few children, so now you can screen many other children like me in the cool shade of your love," Rajshri's voice was stronger now, her sobs heavier.

"Hai Ram!!!" wailed Taru Ma, "What misfortune to get a girl like this? All the time pretending to be a mouse but look, the slightest opportunity and she turns into this *neech,* vixen. What other sorrows will I have to bear in this life?"

"*Bahu!*" Bhimsen raised his index finger at Rajshri unable to restrain himself. He and the girl had not exchanged more than forty words in their two years together under one roof. How could one morning at the fair grounds change all that? "Girl, listen!" he roared.

Rajshri shivered, clutching her *pallu* even more tightly. She had only once had the occasion to talk to her father-in-law directly in her 15 months in this home. That occasion had been a reprimand as well, instigated by Taru Ma. Rajshri felt a loosening of her bladder and tightening in her chest but still she went on, "That's what I do pitaji sir, all the time, I listen. But today I want to tell you something - it's a good thing that I am not allowed to bare my face to you because even if my face were naked all of you would be still blind to its concerns. To you, my eyes are my shame, my veil; its purchased respect. I have hated this veil so much but today this veil feels like a blessing, shielding me from ...."

"Take her inside your room!" Bhimsen turned to Ramesh.

"Saru Chachi! Saru Chachi!" Rajshri sobbed as Ramesh stepped forward, the directive from his father making him suddenly come alive.

Saru Chachi, her eyes still moist, raised her right palm as a parting blessing to Rajshri and was out of sight within five minutes. Everyone in that courtyard thought about Saru Chachi that night. Only Rajshri felt what Saru Chachi might have felt.

*

Inside their locked room, her body contorted in fetal position on her intermittent marital bed, a sobbing Rajshri asked Ramesh, "Will you hit me now?"

"You should not have spoken to pitaji like this," Ramesh said. "It's all the influence of Saru Chachi. Rajshri sat up and looked at him directly; his skin still had the softness of an adolescent, his eyes held a hint of luminosity, all set in a face that mirrored his father's.

"It's a girl," Rajshri said.

Ramesh arched his eyebrows, paused and then said, "The world needs girls as well."

Then he opened the rusted steel alimirah parked near the mouth of the door, and handed Rajshri her first birthday gift from his own salary. A sheer red *chunari* sari, the fabric crinkled chiffon, the red vibrant and bonded with silver stars on green-yellow tie and die speckles. Rajshri fingered the fabric, gazing at the stars peeping in from the metal barred window, while Ramesh brought her water from the earthen pitcher lying next to the bed. The night sky appeared no different from any other night – a blue-black blanket of darkness made bearable by the playful, peeping stars that dared its darkness. The evening's drama precipitated the exhaustion of a long day. Rajshri now felt extremely tired; she placed her hand on her belly and pressed her feet against the bed head stand for relief. Then she threw the loose fabric of the sari on her once-slim frame and brought one end of it over her head, stopping right at the junction of the eyes and the nose. The room was suddenly bathed in a red fragrant light, the stars seeming to fade away.

Metro

The Delhi Metro had been around for two years, just a quarter year less than their engagement. Tomorrow would be the day she would ride it for the first time. Tomorrow, a day that would make itself unforgettable. She did not know it then. Theirs had been a long engagement. They had wanted it to be that way. She'd written her last exam at the university three weeks ago. Post her examinations, for the first few days she'd felt odd, not knowing how or with what to replace the frenetic energy of exam preparation. But today, sitting across him on this not-so-big table, she felt light. Ready to dive into preparing for their life together; a life that would begin formally in four weeks, once they were married. But those are matters of the past and the future. It is the present where everything happens and therefore deserving of our focus.

He appeared altered to her that morning. Unusually chatty among other things. "It's hard to study once you are married," he said as she sipped her coffee. She nodded. They were glad her exams were behind them. She was still undecided on what to do next. They figured they could both use a short break to kick-start their married life. He was apologetic that they were sitting across each other at Mc Donald's. *I could have sworn there was a nice café here the last time I was here.* She really didn't understand why but nodded anyway. It was bad coffee. Hot, cloudy, less milky than she was used to and made worse by the absence of something solid to go with it. She didn't want to eat a burger in front of him with all the mayo, mustard and ketchup resembling the colours of the Spring festival *holi* on her pretty cream chikaan-work kurta. But now she just felt silly and hungry picking at her French Fries. Then a new song came on in the background – it was Roxette – Center of the Heart and she forgot all about her sandwich craving. They were meeting this time after almost four months. He'd just finished his training in Singapore; it had taken him away for three and half months and while he'd wanted to meet her right after he was back, he waited ten days in order that it not appear inappropriate. They did meet the evening he arrived from Singapore at the Indira Gandhi airport, but you know, with that much family all around, what could you possibly say to each other? He was grateful to see her today; still he did not like the fact that he had to constantly put himself in a supplicant position in front of his future father-in-law in order that he get to see her. She's done with coffee. The fries she will throw away.

"Some shopping?" he asked. She arched her eyebrows knowing how uncomfortable he had looked when her future mother-in-law had taken them shopping for engagement rings and outfits.

"Really?" she replied.

"Really."

They walked a few minutes farther ahead Janpath. To the street facing stores.

"Maybe I'll get a skirt."

It wasn't easy to choose. So many colours and styles. Floral wraparounds, short village belle type, or the long cascading crinkled type. She was undecided between a satrangi tie and dye crinkled variety and another dual shaded long skirt. He agreed that the colours were indeed very bright. The shopkeeper insisted that she, "sister", as he called her, try the skirt over her jeans and so she raised her arms and he gently unfurled the fabrics over her body. Once. Then again. It was a good suggestion; she looked fetching in each one. He - her guy - kept standing patiently at the corner of the store. She looked at him, he at her.

She settled for a pink and yellow skirt with little bullion roses, criss crossing the velvet border at the skirt bottom after bargaining for it just a little bit. She knew she could have gotten it for much lower but she didn't want him to think that she was heartless. And yet she did not want him to think that one could be careless with money. He paid for it. Once they sealed the purchase, she swirled around in her new skirt. The colours and prints of happiness. As she swirled he thought he would much like to see those thin pretty legs hidden under the layers of skirt and jeans. On the way back, in the car, she said, "you will not be so patient with shopping later."

"I will always be patient," he said, not taking his eyes off the steering. He'd missed her so much in Singapore. But it had not been as easy for her; it had taken her many months to trust love but unexpectedly today she felt this intimacy with him that she'd not felt earlier. Suddenly, she felt that if he asked her for anything, there would be nothing she could refuse him. In fact, he wouldn't even have to ask. The joy – it felt similar to the feeling one gets when, after searching for long on the radio, you find the channel playing the song you need. They were nearing her parents' home in Dwarka, a suburb that no longer felt like a satellite town, also her home for the next four weeks, and traffic was not sparse but not too tight too. She pressed a button; the car glass window folded and hid itself allowing the breeze on her face. He took her hand in his – she didn't bother to turn her face to meet his eyes, and kept looking outside. An ardor inside the two of them, simmering for so long, finally finding a place to unburden itself. When they entered her second floor apartment, everyone was home. The women, her mother, sister-in-law and fourteen-month old nephew and her other two men – her father and her brother. Our new lovers, they'd absentmindedly kept on holding hands through the elevator. Now inside the home, he took his time to release her hand from his grip. When his eyes met those of the senior man, he said, "I'm sorry to be so late sir." Her father stayed silent for what seemed a while, but it really was just three minutes. The father stood as he spoke, straightening the cotton of his kurta pyjama, "It no longer matters whether it is late or early," the words accompanied by the flicker of a smile on his face. Everyone around her father took a deep breath in, almost as if someone had infused a fresh, bountiful stock of oxygen in the room. He, the man, who had caused this tremor, continued to look unflappable.

It was dinner time. Everyone was seated appropriately around the still-like-new table; it had been bought especially for their engagement; to entertain the future groom and his family. If you viewed the setting from the ceiling fan you could see all the silver thalis still un-littered by food making a tight rectangle on the table with the various foods in the center. So nicely arranged. Just like him and her. At night after everyone had retired, she lay in bed and re-lived the events of day and blushed, blushed. Yes, it is hard to study after you are married. There are several things that call upon your attention. Responsibilities of the home. Of new family. To each other. And Sex. What must it feel like? What must it feel like to take your clothes off in front of someone? Allow someone to come so close. Even if you did not want to allow, did you have that choice?

The next morning it was her brother who suggested they go for some "big time shopping" holding out a wad of his bonus that he'd only just cashed last evening from the ATM. She got so excited that she left the chick pea batter she was mixing for bread pakoras half-way and her stirring spoon (she couldn't find the big steel one she usually used and was making do with a teaspoon instead) – that spoon drowned in the batter. Once it drowned in the mixture, there were no more reminders of its presence. No silhouette. No jutting pointy steel tip. But she is not drowning just yet, she is buoyant. "Yes, Yes, Yes," she said, letting her sister-in-law take the cash from her brother. Then she remembered there were all these big sales at Connaught Place (even though that commercial hub now has a new name, Rajiv Chowk, she prefers call it by her parents choice of name), and her sister-in-law concurred that it was boring to shop so close to home always. It was okay to travel a little further. Her sister-in-law, not having too many opportunities to be a girl she once was, wanted to be out for longer. No fun in doing everything for a purpose, everything with speed, alacrity. But later, even upon deep introspection it would remain unclear whose idea it was to take the Metro. Each one would think that it came from her.

What prompted their decision to ride the Metro? Was it her sister-in-law's desire to be a girl for one day after what she'd seen between two people at the dinner table last night? Or her desire to go back to the same places as yesterday, to make the perfect more perfect, or her brother's broken Santro, the one that he'd been neglecting to take to the body shop? Whose idea was it to take the Metro? No one's really. Maybe it was just meant to be.

She was the first one to use the bath. She shaved in the shower, the shaving foam spread on her legs, the water dripping from the shower. She liked the sensation of water falling on her head, half-drowning in it, half-enjoying it. Standing in one place only the hands moving up and down the leg, almost forgetting to breathe till one was forced to remember. The blade gave away. From inside the bathroom she called out to her sister-in- law for a new razor. But sister-in-law was busy massaging the baby.

"Chal na, you can take care of it tomorrow, after all who is going to see you today!"

So she quickly tidied up. Only one leg shaved and kind of bristly, the other more natural with thin, fine black hair all over. The sister-in-law gave the baby a quick bath. The aunt, which would be her, dressed the baby, tidied the room for baby to sleep in. Then she put on the baby a pair of socks – the baby was growing, these socks were almost tight, so she put to fingers inside the baby's socks to loosen them. Stretch them out. She felt happy when she did that, giving comfort before the discomfort became apparent. The last thing she did before she left the house was to place two of the baby's presents from his six-month birthday, a big Winnie the Pooh and a smaller Winnie albeit in a different color (red - orange and a cream - blue) in the bigger Winnie's lap. She set them both on the window parapet, to look outside at the world and enjoy. As they sat in the rickshaw that was about to take them to the Metro station, she felt a tease around the nose. Perhaps it meant a cold was on its way.

The Metro ride from Dwarka to Rajiv Chowk was wonderful. Such clean seats, such comfort. Yes, there were many people on the Metro, but they'd been lucky to find seats. She saw two trains go past each other and made a mental list of the order in which they would comb the stores. Occasionally she and her sister-in-law chatted a little.

Like all bad things it happened very quickly; it is the good things in life that take time. She got off safely from the train and soon made their way to the stairs. At the same time, two men came rushing headlong along the platform. One behind the other. The one giving the chase not particularly fast or rowdy, only agitated. The one being chased - fast, careless. She would learn later that it was case of pick pocketing. One moment she was walking, seven steps away from the stairs, another moment she'd fallen on the tracks. She could feel the bones snap, crack, the moment she fell. Fortunately for her, although several times later she would rail against that seeming good fortune; there had been no moving train on that track. She was conscious till she was placed in the ambulance. She registered everything – the shock, her sister-in-law's screams, the people running in different directions to get help, someone on his cell calling for an ambulance, two military men jumping down the tracks, lifting her above the tracks, making sure not to press on her bloody right leg, long, long before the ambulance and the stretcher got there.

When the doctor who took off her bloody churidar looked at her legs – the right one - its bones smashed and bloody, but with patches of untrammeled skin clinging to the exposed bone and streaming blood - he noticed that it had been shaved. Unlike the other leg that was still intact. And unshaved. All the doctors in the break room agreed that it was bizarre to have so many fine irreparable fractures all coalescing into one big broken shard and that they'd never seen a case like this before. Of course, it would have to be cleaned, waited upon to see if it might spring any secondary infections. Only the young doctor who was pouring himself coffee in that very same break room felt angry that a young girl's confidence at leaving one leg unshaved for a day had been shattered. For her, every moment at the hospital in the first three days had a sweet, floaty quality about it. After *the* moment of inevitable decision making, after her brother whispered in her ear about the leg and she nodded only half-comprehending, she mostly drifted in and out of sleep. With much the same entitlement that a child enters her parents' bedroom in the middle of the night. He came to see her. He cried. She knew it was him because of that teardrop which fell on her forehead and she could recognize its source even with her eyes shut.

Everyone was at the table when she took to her crutches for the first time. The crutches were not heavy, almost stylish. Light green, the colour her sister-in-law would remember from the colour of the lehngas that they had been debating the past weekend. The sister-in-law had picked out these crutches. Happy to do the dirty work, relieved to be away from the eyes of her family, but it would be a short lived relief. Because no matter where one goes, you go with yourself.

She looked at her right leg, the pyjama flapping unmoored under the whirring of the ceiling fan and she thought, she thought of her missing leg. This thing that had lived with her and grown with her. That had been around all the time. Swelling during long hours of examination study, cramping during RUN For the ENVIRON marathons, waiting patiently with toes spread for mehndi, for pedicures, for flaming red nail polish. This leg she'd never bothered to thank while it helped stretch, reach, and press for the accelerator. This leg now gone. Now whatever be the kind of day this void would be her constant companion. This missingness. This thing that once was and would now never be again.

In the days that will follow, mostly well meaning people will drop by, and give her advice like *pain is compulsory, suffering is optional*. Over and over people will offer her answers to her unspoken questions, all answers she does not and will not like. Sometimes she will try to explain to people what it means to be her, but soon enough she will learn to withdraw in silence when she discovers its futility; like the futility of telling a child the secrets of an adult. The world wants to be young and pretty and she is young and pretty, but over and over she will be reminded that no, not her kind of young. Or her kind of pretty. She will be reminded day after day that life is a never ending exam. But that is still farther away. Right now, right now they at the table, all together. Sitting at the chair beside the dining table, she thinks of him, the missing link, first. He would want to go on. Marry her. Fulfill unspoken promises. Her once designated future mother-in-law will hesitate in giving them her blessings (*if she cannot bring good luck to herself what would she bring them, their family?*), but his father will stand shoulder to shoulder with the boy in his intention. She can see it all. He, the man who has the seeds of everything, both rebellion and deference in him, what would he choose? But it didn't matter whatever be his choice. Either way, their lives were changed forever. Just because of a stupid leg. She thought of him, what would it feel like to show someone your stump, a story that was once promised an end? Now that she had lost something old, would nothing new ever knock on her life? Would she ever walk without stumbling? What would it mean to walk without a leg? And it would be a long, long time before she would concede that life was a song, so what if it be a sad song for some. For now, she just looked at her family, barring one, almost family, her eyes moving from one and landing on the other and back again.

They are still at the table. In her father's eyes she can see despair, like the fogginess that comes upon truck driver who has been driving all night and now? Now what? Now he has been derailed, his consignment desecrated just before delivery; this driver, he is tired, very tired. In her brother's eyes she sees determination, he has a list ready in his mind - perhaps the Jaipur foot, the best hospitals in the country and if that fails, a stamp on his sister's passport. In her sister-in-law's eyes she sees unease akin to the unease women often express when being seen by a male gynecologist. So closed. Not allowing examination. Not allowing healing. Then there is her nephew. She is his favorite and she knows that. Why must she search him? His eyes? When searching, search thoroughly, everywhere. There is nothing in her nephew's eyes. Since the day she took the Metro, except Winnie big and small Winnie staring out at the world from his bedroom window, nothing has been the same for her little nephew either. Since her accident he has spent a lot of time with the neighbors. He has had to cry for his meals; meals no longer chase him like they once used to. But she finds nothing in his eyes. They are clear like the sky. But this search has not been fruitless, even if it be to discover what one already knows. There *is* one pair of eyes which reflect back to her everything that she holds in her heart. That pair of eyes belongs to her mother. For her there is no relief at this discovery, she has known it in her body since birth, but it is a rediscovery nonetheless. So for now, for now, it is enough to just put everything aside, and bury her face in the tummy she'd once lived in as a tenant and just cry, cry.

Auntyji

She's back. The girl at the health club front desk with Auntyji's eyes. Always wide in unspoken anticipation. Her third left finger has a tiny, shiny new rock. Today is a Saturday. An off day. A day for leisure. For *Great America*. Auntyji has been dead exactly a year today. Auntyji. I didn't need to see her alive to find her everywhere.

If everything goes as it should, by tonight, I too, will have my very own shiny bling to admire in the soft pink light of my night lamp. I will then be released from Auntyji's spell. In Great America. Between swings that take me high and low, I will find firm ground. Soon I will have everything Auntyji wanted – once for herself, then for me. Ma says that it was I who found Auntyji. I, who cemented the family's ties with her. I, who crawled into her open-for-the-bhajiwali apartment door and hoisted myself straight onto her fish tank. That 1968 August morning, Auntyji got more than free dhania-mirchi to garnish her signature paneer-koftas in tomato-cream sauce. Auntyji got herself a fief.

Why did Ma have to seek Auntyji when she had a sister and sister's family to share a life with? Ma says that in those early days - those long, lonely days before her sister Usha and brother-in-law Dinesh entered our world with baby Ketaki – afternoons became synonymous with inexplicable despair. She knew that the woman who lived in the apartment across the hallway had the habit of keeping her apartment door open in the mornings; might that reflect the state of this woman's heart as well? Ma, newly emboldened by loneliness, would set me down day after day and let me crawl across the hallway to Auntyji's apartment. She tells me this with the reverence that becomes our voices when we reminiscent about life-changing events for kindness offered during adversity is not easily forgotten.

"Did you sweep-mop the walkway between the apartments for me?" I ask. Ma looks at me as if I am crazy. How Auntyji might have heard the faint thumps of an eleven-month old is beyond me; but Ma always got chai, sometimes freshly cooked beaten rice pohe or just plain old crunchy moong dal khakhra, an occasional sari and plenty of free babysitting. Auntyji and I spent hours looking at the fishes. As I learned to talk, I'd ask questions - why does this fishy keep its mouth open all the time? Why that fishy hiding behind grey rocks always? Why does that one looks sad sad? Where the purple fishy we got last week? Ma says that her answers were inventive, tightroping honesty and hope…so *that it is ready when food arrives …because it is not sure of whom to show itself to… it is wondering when its orange friend will come to play… sometimes we are afraid for no reason...It's gone to another being with the same name as mine for a vacation.*

I do not remember any of it. Here is what I remember.

Auntyji was younger than Usha Masi but Naveen, Auntyji's son, was older to me by three years. There was not a single birthday till the year I took that flight to New York that Auntyji did not bake a cake for me. She gave me and Ketaki hot, scalding baths and rubbed us spotless while Ma packed a diaper bag for an enormous and more-than-ready Usha Masi. I remember that she put me in big girl scarf dupattas at six and bras at 12. That Mayank, Usha Masi's second child, was her favorite amongst all four of us children and she unfailingly gave him head champi massages until he was six and a quarter, every alternate day. Up until the day he fell from the balcony. *All this* I remember. But most of all, I remember Auntyji for the force of her tongue.

Even in a country like India where bonds between strangers are easily formed and when under attack display the resilience of the hepatitis virus, Auntyji, Ma and Usha Masi stood out in their devotion to each other. People often mistook them for sisters. Ma didn't seem to mind the assumption; still it was apparent to me even at that young age that it was only after Mayank's birth that Usha Masi welcomed Auntyji into the fold. Mayank's death sealed Auntyji's position. Auntyji lost no time appropriating powers. *Poonam don't walk the streets in that frock! Poonam red lipsticks are for you– know-who and Poonam please serve chai in a tray, not like that! Poonam don't laugh with your mouth so wide open, boys will get the wrong signal. Poonam, Poonam, don't, don't.*

Auntyji whose hair always smelt of mogra and jasmine, who wore long sari blouses with sleeves that sat under the elbow. Auntyji married at eighteen to a mother-less man, the most versatile cook in our housing society, Auntyji the this, Auntyji the that. Auntyji the self-styled upholder of feminine virtue and conduct. Auntyji my protector. Was Auntyji my emancipator or my repressor? Everyone seemed to think one way. My most recurring memory of Auntyji is of being reprimanded by her. Her tone was always the same degree of sharp, shaming, bitter - regardless of the nature of the misdemeanor; curiously neither my mother nor my aunt ever intervened in my defense. Ketaki, three years my junior was never in any position to help. Only Naveen - Auntyji's Naveen would offer quiet support - a surreptitious glass of water to silence tears, a cup of tea to soothe the shame. I remember that I lost count of the movies I gave up because of Auntyji or the number of strangers who heard her paraphrase my *situation*, "It's *not* acne, it's jawani oozing from her pores. Keep careful eye on that fire, I'd say." And she did her part. But Auntyji was smart. She sent out the right signals when someone, anyone was watching. Always adding an icing of honey to the dish. Once on an especially long bus ride from Kalbadevi to Bandra, a stranger who had been watching us for a while, winked appreciatively before he got off, his kind bespectacled face breaking into a unfettered smile at my good fortune, "You are lucky to have someone watch out for you like that little girl," he said to me after he was done smiling the Great Wall of smiles. Yes sir, I was lucky. Bloody lucky.

Auntyji's eyes never left my back (and Ketaki's to a lesser degree) and they burnt every boy who ever crossed our threshold merely to pick up homework. We were convinced that Auntyji hated us. Me more than Ketaki; why we were not sure. It was all bearable while we had Naveen. But Naveen was a prodigy. It is fate that prodigies leave the nest behind quickly. I on the other hand seemed glued to my parents' nest. Did I not know how to fly? Or did I not have wings? I never had time to think about anything other than Auntyji. The same thoughts played themselves over and over in my head: *Why don't you let me live Auntyji? And why do you have such a hold on those who hold the keys to that life? Why don't you let me live, Auntyji?*

*

Why must I remember Auntyji now that I am under no obligation to suffer her presence? Why must I tell each person I love her story? How can I forget her? She is there in every frame of my story. I am unable to live without Auntyji's ghost presence. Usha Masi would never tire of reminding us of the power of physical presence - *Chaar din ek gali ka kutta bhi aas paas phire to woh bhi apna ho jata hai.* But unlike Usha Masi's mythical street dog, who might find room in your heart just by sticking around, Auntyji never found a clean well lit corner in my heart. I never learnt to love her. My body experienced such release each time she left the room. Auntyji was intolerable; only three people seemed to disagree. But even they sent conflicting signals.

"Did you see Sharad Babu's crushed face when she cancelled his plans to visit Naveen over Holi?" said Usha Masi.

"Mother was right - a fire-tongued woman is her household's blessing and her husband's curse," said Ma.

They looked just like Ketaki and me when they giggled. I took my chance. "Why do you talk to her if you hate her so much?" I asked Ma. She tightened immediately. *You are never to speak about Auntyji like that ever again and **I** don't hate her.*

Auntyji had a dream team of three. Sharad Babu, the husband, Ma and Usha Masi. Sharad Babu – Papa appended that suffix after learning that he had graduated from Presidency College in Calcutta and the name stuck. Till the end, even in his new building everybody called him Sharad Babu. Sharad Babu was true to his name. Ice man. The more fire Auntyji spewed on him, the more readily this unflappable ice-man lit his incense sticks. So much so that whenever my nose picks the hint of incense, I am convinced Sharad Babu will step out of a door somewhere. Sure, there's a small logistical glitch - he's been dead a decade - but light an aromatic stick and I'll wait anyway.

Sharad Babu was an early riser. He would unlock the apartment door soon after his morning cuppa and leave it ajar for the rest of the morning. For air. Those mornings, I could adjust any two clocks by the occurrence of two mutually independent events; Ma's setting of piping bournvita flavored milk and green chili spiked potato parathas on our dining table for Papa and Dinesh Uncle, and Sharad Babu's recitation of Vishnu Stotra would be exactly 15 minutes apart. Even from behind a closed door it was a treat to listen to Sharad Babu's voice - each Sanksrit syllable intimate, perfect, distinct –*ShantakaramBhujangsayanam Padamanbhan… Shantakaram …* "Why must you open the door so early? I can hear the sweeper woman's noises!" There was not a single day she let him complete the chant in one go. But he kept on. If I close my eyes I can see him clearly. He is wearing a white dhoti, a dhoti he will discard soon in favor of a cotton-linen work pant, maybe dirty green or navy blue. He wears a white windbreaker, a ganji, with a white linen and dark pink square checked towel slung over his shoulders. In time, the dark pink of these criss-cross towel lines will spread unevenly on the white base. Eventually he will finish his prayers, wipe his kumkum and sandalwood fingers on his towel. Then the sweat on his forehead. Soon after, his eyes will catch me stepping out – he will wink his left eye at me and ask, "What did Krishna say to Arjuna in the Gita?" Not waiting for me to answer, he will answer for his question differently each morning. My favorite was…*Again and Again He who abides in Me Acts.* Each morning Auntyji made half-hearted advances disguised in irritation, only to be rebuffed by Sharad Babu, albeit gently.

"Why must you open the apartment door so early?" to which Sharad Bbabu would respond with such tenderness in his voice, "We need the fresh air Naveen's mother."

When I was in 9th grade after I'd heard this exchange for almost six months intermittently, it occurred to me that doors didn't need to be closed for love to be expressed. Couldn't Auntyji see that? But clearly she couldn't - there were days when the brief morning exchange between husband and wife would be enough for my antennae to perk up. I'd especially stay away those days; but those evenings Auntyji would come see Ma and find me somehow. I envied Auntyji's fishes. At least they got to die. Get away one final time. Auntyji's fishes kept dying every few weeks. She kept getting them back. Once when things were hard, she sold her favorite ring for her fishes. She was curiously luminous that day. I foolishly hoped that her new-found ease would spill into the week. But how thin can an elephant get? I chafed under Auntyji's reign. Longed for someone to liberate me. It never occurred to me that I could do it myself.

I was eighteen, Ketaki almost sixteen when twenty-something Girish arrived. Girish was to be our guest for four odd weeks. But we had two girls and not enough room, hence he camped at Sharad Babu's in the evenings.

"Yes, that's best Dinesh Saab, who knows how long it takes to find a decent teaching position? Why put milk in front of a cat and then lament its loss?" said Papa.

Sharad Babu nodded pleasantly. Cats, milk - all the world was the same to him.

As soon as we heard his name, we wanted so much to fall in love with Girish. For him to liberate us. Me more than Ketaki. But he turned out to be something else.

Girish looked just like I'd imagined him. But I stopped imagining the moment he opened his mouth. Girish was awkward. Broken sentences, faraway glances, many gestures of the hand. But when he talked about books something came over him. When he talked about Shakespeare he further transformed. Girish used our dining table chair for a rocking chair. He rocked back and forth wearing white Bata flip-flops with blue handles, reading Tolstoy one day and Dickens the following day. I kept waiting for him to fall, to get so locked in the rhythm of the prose that he lost his balance. Girish never lost his rhythm. He never fell.

*

I have been single a little over five years now. In the faint light of the bedside lamp, each night that I share my bed with Romi I worry that I have become Auntyji. *Don't bare your arms and legs at the same time! Don't stay out too late on rainy evenings. Don't hang out with boys that don't make good grades.*

I am relentless in my diktats. It is inevitable that Romi, despite her patience will hit back one day. *You are a Don't machine.* The words spill out Romi of like they've been friends a long time. There is no force in delivery. No Mother prefixed or suffixed. Romi breaks no more rules; she needs no more reminders. I back off. We live in an uncomfortable truce.

Last year this day I met Nick for the first time. Two months later Auntyji died. Even though Nick and

I had nothing on each other at that time, somehow, I carried his picture with me. A group photo, of course, I'm not that stupid. Ketaki, my cousin, now a mother of two is still my best friend, my confidante. And now she reads me even on occasions I do not wish to be read.

Do secrets, when shared, bring strength or shame? Ketaki and I have shared so many secrets. Each secret I tell Ketaki brings me strength, a lightness. She listens. Then forgets. Then another day mines the secret for a nugget, a gem I have willfully discarded. "He looks like Girish," remarked Ketaki as she glanced through the current crop of photos I'd carried with me home.

"Who?" I asked, pretending not to understand.

"Your new guy," she said with a quiet smile.. "He's not mine yet," I said, "And no he doesn't look like Girish."

"He will be soon," said Ketaki.

And we fell quiet.

I tell her how I found him, this single father of two boys, almost by chance. Ballet Class. To drop off his sister's daughter. He was standing at the far end of the room and he pried open my heart with one glance. Two weeks later he showed up at my manicurist's, his surgeon fingers extending a lost pair of sunglasses which were not mine. Ketaki listens with a calm attention that is just her, without condescension, but off-late I have started detecting a whiff of pity mingled in this attention. I can't say I begrudge her that; but that it is there makes me angry. Holding back hurts her, hurts me, so I swallow this pity with everything else.

Ketaki wears starched cotton salwar kameezes now. Our balance of power has shifted in her favor. She lives in a marriage that has only a hint of passion and two full servings of commitment. She has not been greedy. Therefore, she has more. Unlike me. I am usually angry with Ketaki whenever we are together in India. But she redeems herself the moment I fly out. The moment I land on American shores.

On the airplane I examine the photograph again. My eyes sit on Nick's face, his glasses, his hands around the three children and I can slowly begin to see the resemblance Ketaki could immediately spot. The same tilt of the head, that same longish fingers, the arch of the brow, the high cheekbones.

I look at the chocolate shade on my nails and am suddenly gripped by such a longing to be with Nick. The seat belt sign is lightedbut not before the airhostess brings me the coffee and a sandwich I'd asked for almost a half hour ago. The turbulence makes us shake, I drink the black liquid quickly, afraid that it might spill over me and the two laptops flanking me.

I miss Nick. But besides Ketaki there is someone else I want to show Nick off to – I wish I could find Girish, accost him on a busy street when he is lost in thought and say, "See! I found you at last," I want to then tease him with something only I know. But that of course will not happen.

On the airport when we had a quiet moment together, Ketaki asked me *Where is Girish*? I tell him I last heard from him when Romi was six months. Almost fourteen years ago. He'd tracked me down through a common acquaintance after he'd heard that I was now a mother. "Where is he now?" Ketaki asks. I shake my head. Shrug my shoulders. Does she not know that a few Google searches will bring him to us? We don't want to find out. We don't want to admit as much.

*

It is 1982. Colour is about to be introduced in the lives of Indians. The Asian Games will change our television sets from black and white to colour. But it will be no mean trade. Our colour TV set will mean that we go without presents for one Diwali and two birthdays. That bathroom tiles will remain chippy and the wet ceiling precarious for another six months. But no matter, we will do anything for colour. Auntyji was no different.

Girish has been with us almost ten days now. We are out on Chowpatty Beach. Family outing.

There was an ease in being with Girish that made arguments the most natural occurrence. He refused to share his bananas with me. Injured, I refuse to let him sample my tikkhi bhel.

"What will you do if you don't get a teaching job soon?" asked Ketaki. Waves crashed all around us. A group of children around us played with balloons that didn't have too much air in them. A young couple sharing a rice puff bhel puri looked up from their snack at us in half amusement, half-irritation at the urgency of our strides. We were walking faster even without realizing it. Ma and Usha Masi had fallen back, only Auntyji kept pace.

"Why not meet tomorrow when tomorrow comes?" said Girish.

Auntyji nodded in agreement. Then he turned to her and told her he adored her fishes. "You take such good care of them," he said, his brows furrowed. That was his smile. Auntyji blinked and gave him a half-smile. She appeared strangely docile when she was with him, constantly tugging at her hair and at the loose drape of her sari pallav. Girish appeared eager to please, attentive and nodded approvingly at all opinions expressed by her, regardless of the quality of those opinions. I wanted to grab his collar and throw his glasses in the sand and tell him, "You idiot, I am the biggest fish in her fish bowl. Good to see. Not fit to eat. Only fit to die. *And No One Takes Good Care of Me!*" Of course, I didn't tell him. I never did what I wanted to then.

I should have told him. I had many opportunities. Girish took good care of us. Of me. He expounded and explained Shakespeare till we were forced to concede his relevance. Laughed at our humorless, complicated jokes. Refused to take slight even when insult was intended. We taught him curse words in Marathi and told him they were polite greetings. Challenged him to Energie drinking three-way matches. I always won. One time, the vendor did not have enough strawberry flavors to propel my victory; Girish and Ketaki drank only three bottles of their pista-flavored milk. Within eight days, Papa and Dinesh Uncle were wondering why they'd bothered Sharad Babu and Auntyji. Girish had made them gender blind. By day ten, everyone felt so safe with him that we were even allowed to take him around by ourselves. Auntyji joined us on all those trips. To Papa and Dinesh Uncle, Girish could have been one of us. Except that he wasn't.

The night before *the* moment, I fought with Girish. Something trivial. He tried to make up. "Come now, Poonam, let's go eat some bhel puri. Tikkhi for you. Sev Puri for me and Ketaki. My treat," he said.

"Yes, Poonam hurry! Who knows how long our itinerant bhelwaala will stick to the same spot."

I shook my head.

"Why?" he asked. I looked at my besan-flour and mustard oil stained kurta and said stupidly, "I am not looking pretty today."

"You'll look the same tomorrow," he said, his eyes steady on mine. Everyone in the room laughed. I forgave him and changed for bhel.

That evening I understood Girish. And from then I used what I know.

*

It was Ketaki who saw it all. No one was prepared, except me. Definitely not Auntyji. It is around 6:30 am on a peak summer morning; the sun will soon overstay its welcome but we are not there yet. The monsoons are technically five weeks away. Auntyji is in the bath after prepping the kitchen for Shanta bai, our common maid. Meanwhile Girish is up. He hasn't been able to sleep all night because of the incessant traffic, small town bungalow-boy that he is; last night was particularly noisy. Auntyji steps out of the bathroom, her face patted dry but rapidly getting wet in a new way. If you entered the bath soon after Auntyji, it would smell of jasmine oil, turmeric, sandalwood, shikakai hair soap – each fragrance distinct yet uncloying. She always came out fully clothed. Unlike Ma or Usha Masi who stepped out in their petticoats and blouses and wore their saris in front of Ketaki or me or our respective fathers. *How does she do it*, we'd wonder. Wear a sari in a wet bathroom and stay dry. That question had lingered in our consciousness adding to the legend-horror of Auntyji. Up until that morning Ketaki actually entered the bathroom soon after Auntyji and found a dry square of almost 20 x 20 inches. 20 x 20. That was all she'd needed.

Girish was reading the newspaper, drinking Shanta bai's handmade tea when Auntyji stepped out of the bath. Ketaki was there too, waiting to entrust Auntyji with Ma's rice kheer before make a dash for school. Upon Auntyji's entry, Girish's eyes did not find their way back to *The Hindustan Times* editorial, instead they lingered on her face. Unblinkingly. Unaware of his gaze, Auntyji loosened the towel braided around her hair to expose what lay underneath. Endless waves of perfumed black hair. Ketaki thought that Girish might smile. He didn't. His eyes simply surveyed all of Auntyji's face like our archaeologist fathers surveyed old rocks. Their concentration was their love. When her eyes met Girish's that morning Auntyji discovered that doors did need not be closed for love to be expressed. And remembered that she was once a young girl, who had been married off early.

*

Happiness! An exclamation mark changes everything. A decade and a half ago, fresh out of school, between apartments, subways and an unending stack of files I'd spy three exclamation marks on my way to work. It would have made such good copy if I'd told my bosses. Brought me that coveted promotion. Instead I stayed greedy. Kept those three exclamation marks safe in my heart. The power of those three stenciled marks on a hand-cart becoming accentuated in the rain and snow. *Rest! Coffee! Tamales*! Lousy tamales but I bought them anyway. Ate them anyway. My palate was not trained to waste like my American daughters' and her friends. Their doughnut faces not hardwired to stick with the lousy. They never ask … w*hat if* I ate this? What if I listened to someone? They only chose, chose, chose.

When Romi was two, an elevator door got stuck and I asked a woman I'd known three weeks a simple question. *Where do you work?* Sixty-five seconds later a door opened. Sixteen months and seven flights later, California! And Elevators!! I recommend question asking.

After her last head bath, Auntyji glowed like a woman blessed with the shine of love. She no longer wore her hair in a bun. Instead it had come loose and with it many other things. She threw spices fearlessly on sautéed vegetables. Her saris morphed from cotton mangalgiris to chiffons and gorgettes, the colours no longer dark, bold but now soft, light.

"Where did all these saris come from suddenly?" Ketaki asked. We didn't know. We just knew that she was wearing them now. She was more generous with her smiles. Even with me. Her guard was down. But only when Ketaki woke me up at 6 am one Saturday morning that I realized how down was down.

"Poonam, wake up, wake up! Auntyji has shaved her legs!"

"What rubbish!" I exclaimed.

"*Sacchi!* It's true," Ketaki said. I glared at her disbelievingly. Crestfallen Ketaki swore several times. On herself. On me. And I still remember the translucency of Ketaki's neck fold as she pinched it between her right thumb and forefinger to certify the veracity of her statement like it happened yesterday. We lured Auntyji to a game of street cricket with the building boys and Girish. She was easy prey. Girish was the bowler. He was good in alternate balls. Auntyji hit one of his bad balls for a four. She ran. The boy who was her opposing batsman ran too. The sari folds felt heavy as she ran; she lifted a few of her sari pleats along with her petticoat and bunched them at the top tucking them snug in the drawstring near her navel. Legs had indeed been shaved. Girish clean bowled her in the next ball. She pretended to be angry. He pretended to be apologetic. They both laughed for real. The rain broke our game. As I saw Auntyji walk up the dingy staircase I noticed that her greenish gray eyes were sparkling like the rain water that was collecting itself all around us. Not muddy, not yet. Girish had detected a fragrance, but everyone was now bathed in its scent.

Later at night, when everyone had long retired, Ketaki and I stood out looking the balcony holding two cheap cups with chai dregs in one and cola in another.

"Auntyji has become very ..."

"Free....," I completed the sentence for Ketaki.

She nodded. We'd stopped short of using that word, even though we both knew what it was. We were no different from men who undressed us with their eyes at street corners.

*

How does one cement her place in a man's heart? Is the way through his mind, through his stomach, through his balls? I once ensnared a man, the kind of man that donates sperm and last names, that kind of man – and sidled close to him under neon ladies room lights and placed his hands on my waist. First one, then another. One higher than the other. In fingertip distance of my right breast. He did nothing for almost a minute. The longest sixty seconds of my life.

"What Poonam?" he asked.

"What do you think Eric?"

He said nothing, did nothing. Later took me home to his mother. I still long for his mother. When I miss her too much I search for her in my daughter. The way to a man's heart is definitely not through his mother.

Auntyji tried all of them. And everybody succeeds once in a while. Girish's appreciated food like no one we'd seen before. Ketaki and I routinely ate Auntyji's fare without much fuss. Not Girish. Everything was big deal. "Krishnaji you have a way with spices. Even your karelas taste sweet."

Ma and Usha Masi sat vaguely uncomfortable and frozen at the far end of the table, while Auntyji blushed, wearing a white sari with red flowers that criss-crossed her buttocks and thighs. Soon Ketaki and I were belching, having pigged out eating the chole. Auntyji didn't eat them. She stayed pristine. The men saw none of it. Their rocks, fossils and balance sheets kept them busy. I knew she was coming after me when she started singing my favorite songs.

I want to see you till my heart is content

I hope my heart is never content

I was counting the hours the day she wore my favorite colours. The same colours of the picture over the fishes. Blue and white soft kota cotton with light blue on its borders, the colours favored by the goddess of learning. *Yes, Auntyji, it's a good idea to give Girish a few books as a welcome present. No Auntyji Flora Fountain is not a good place for Russian writers. I know where to find them.*

If Auntyji was surprised at my easy acceptance she did not show it. Girish had blunted her radar. I coached her on the salient features distinguishing each author. After a long time, *I* had made Auntyji happy. Girish had an interview in the morning and was not expected back until late afternoon. Auntyji busied herself scrubbing the dried film of chai cream skin that Girish would pluck like a harp player and plant on the circumference of the mouth of the tea cup. She was now wearing a sleeveless blouse. She'd changed into it after Sharad Babu left for work. Ma and Usha Masi did not show any emotion when they saw her bare arms. I kept looking at her arms every chance I got, the small pox immunization depression riveting almost like it was a piece of ornamentation in itself.

Girish was ecstatic. It was my idea that Auntyji take full credit. *This is limited edition. And this, this one – I've wanted it for the longest time.* Soon he was speechless with gratitude. And whatever Girish was, Auntyji was too. Soon the buoyancy of her own feelings became overwhelming for her. She let him loose in the evening; maybe she was tired, maybe she wanted to contain her feelings just enough that they would not spill out in front of Sharad Babu.

As soon as I heard the doorbell ring, I ran into Ma's bedroom and flopped on her bed. When Girish knocked on Ma's door, Ketaki did her part. Ketaki did not let him in; she spoke to him in whispers thorough the ajar door.

"She's very tired Girish. Nothing much, just the exhaustion of preparing for the upcoming finals. Yes, maybe tomorrow we can go for a walk together."

As Girish turned to leave, I said to Ketaki in a drowsy monotone, "Can you massage my feet another time Ketu? I had no idea I'd have such a bad day with bus connections while promising Auntyji. If Dostoyevsky came in front of me right now, I'd pull his hair out!"

Everything was faster, tighter after that moment. Girish didn't praise meals anymore. Refused second helpings. I saw him leave early in the mornings as I dried my hair in our balcony that Ketaki and I had shared as play area as children. Girish wouldn't return until late, long after I was back from college.

Auntyji was a fighter. She tried harder. Made more complicated dishes, *You didn't like the malai kofta the other day…here try this new mughlai recipe,* she memorized Tagore's poetry and recited it for us in halting English, offered to massage Girish's tired feet, made headache remedies when he refused chai. But he refused, refused, kept refusing. He left her with very few options.

The layout was like this. Two sofa chairs on either side flanking a longer sofa with a low back. The central piece had an almost divan like appearance and was just a tad longer than the American love seat. A rectangular coffee-table in between these three items. This room we called the drawing room even though it had no drawings. In America, I have learnt to call it the living room, although no one lives there, except credit card debt embedded in upholstery and hidden behind paintings.

Usha Masi and I sat at the dining table peeling boiled potatoes and shelling peas for pav bhaji. Auntyji had closed her kitchen for the afternoon. Ma left us to get chai and refreshments for Girish when he arrived. Girish did not refuse Ma, grabbed the plate full of food with a grateful smile and sat himself on the sofa opposite facing my chair. From where I was sitting I had full view. Usha Masi only partial view. I could sense that the day been harder than usual for Girish. The sun had scorched his face, the sweat still lingered on his crumpled shirt. I felt such a surge of tenderness when he placed his right foot on top his left and used the friction between the two to massage his exhaustion out.

Auntyji entered barefoot. She was wearing a lilac sari with silver thread work on it. She looked exquisite, her hair had been freshly washed, she wore minimal jewelry - a rope of pink pearls around her neck, a single silver bangle on her right hand, two thin payals on her ankles, her lips riveting despite and not because of her cheap lipstick saturated with petroleum jelly. Only the slightly loose mauve-lilac blouse felt off.

She lay down, face buried in the divan-sofa pillows. Girish picked up a newspaper. A piece of bread got stuck in his throat. He pushed it down with a swig of Ma's brown, dark extra-sweet chai. Then she went for it. She turned her face toward the bare wall, drew a few hairs across her face and shrugged half a shoulder. The tottering blouse fell below exposing her right shoulder. It was a beautiful shoulder. Girish did not flinch. He simply got up and walked away.

*

Two weeks ago I spied Nick buying that ring for me while I was out for lunch. I'd imagined this moment so many times, but that I would get to witness it in the making – such relief! Like someone has changed the water in the fish tank of my life. Now there is nothing missing in me. From outside the glass display I could see him looking at each ring intently, examining the diamonds as the store clerk modeled them on her fingers for him. His face is serious, intent. His eyes expectant. I want to charge in, hug him, smother his face with kisses. But I hold back. *It is early for this*; I want to tell him. But I see him, his expression eager, his brows arched and I tell myself, better early than never. We will do it his way. I instinctively know when he will glance in my direction. I run away.

That evening I ask him, "How about we go away for the weekend?"

He laughs. "And who will watch the kids?" "How about Great America?" he says. Yes, I say anywhere you want to take me, high and low. The haze is lifting. I can now see and feel Auntyji's pain clearly. You don't always need to be hit to hurt.

Auntyji did not join us for dinner that evening. Ma served all the husbands – hers and the other two. Usha Masi took a plate of pav bhaji into Auntyji's bedroom and forgot to lock the door behind her. I had been holding my bladder for too long anticipating this possibility. There were three toilets, two small ones and one master one in Auntyji's room. When Sharad Babu went to use the one in guest room, I ran to use the second one in the room opposite Auntyji's.

Later, I stood at the periphery of the bath door hidden from the dining table view. I couldn't see much across through the sliver of space between two doors. I saw saris crumpled and strewn across the terrazzo floor, like someone had flung them across the length of the room and Auntyji sobbing, sobbing. Her face hidden in Usha Masi's cotton sari belly. Her long hair snaking her back.

"Bas Krishna...," said Usha Masi. "Eat something now..."

"Saab Jhoota hai, Usha! Saab Kuch. I just wanted to give Usha, give to someone who..."

I took a step back. Auntyji kept crying, repeating herself, Usha Masi kept stroking her hair, singing Mayank's favorite lullaby. I left when Usha Masi started crying too. I heard them utter Mayank's name several times; breaking their self-imposed rule. I have tried to complete that sentence in my head a million times .... *To someone who wants it, someone who is grateful, someone new*...Someone **who...**? I will never know. Or why Auntyji personified jhooth and used jhoota instead of jhooth?

Auntyji changed after that night. Life had blindsided her. She spent a lot of time by herself. Girish ate mostly at our place. Even slept in our drawing room for two nights when Auntyji had a migraine attack. The following week Girish found employment and a long lost friend with whom he decided to share an apartment. He thanked us and Sharad Babu profusely for our hospitality. Wanted to thank Auntyji.

"Thank you Krishnaji, thank you for everything," he said standing outside Auntyji's door. We thought she'd never open it. She did. Prayers take time, she said. Then smiled. A full smile. A smile like the occasional ones she gifted us, on birthdays, report card days, no emotion. Like he was us. Her hair in a bun. A bun that never came loose again.

There is no way to cement your place in a man's heart. Or a woman's. Except when they let you. Children, as usual, are a different story. Auntyji lived with her ice man for the rest of his life. Auntyji gave up easy. I didn't. What is the merit gained by loving an asshole? So I let him go, dropped the idea of *us* and picked myself up. Wiped the white cloudy fluid running down my inner thighs and douched, douched and douched. But Romi came anyway; she is a persistent girl. Just like her father.

The week after Girish left, all of Auntyji's fishes died. This time she didn't replace them. Auntyji had been forever altered but it would be a while before this change became apparent to everyone. *What change? Kya badalna*? Ketaki would say each time we dressed to go for an evening show, the fear still alive in Keatki's eyes. *No matter how long you step on a dog's tail can you straighten it out?* Turned out that Auntyji had a different kind of tail.

In the end it was not Girish but Auntyji who liberated me. Auntyji gave me wings. Wings that brought me to America. Forms procured after I pilfered some preliminary addresses from the American Library on the day when I was supposed to be looking for

Russian authors would have kept lying unsigned had it not been for her.

"What are those Poonam?"

"They are forms that will make me rule the world."

"Why don't you fill them?"

I kept quiet.

"I'll talk to Ma and Papa," she said easily.

"I will fill them Auntyji, if you bring the fishes back," I said. She nodded, smiled, pointed to Naveen's pen placed at the doorstep of puja ghar.

I asked her at the airport when she'd come to see me off, "Why not bring the fishes back this time Auntyji?"

"I am getting old Poonam," she said, "they were getting hard to maintain." I wondered if she wanted to say, 'I am getting old Poonam, too old to bear seeing them dying.'

Suddenly it didn't seem like such a great idea after all, going away to a new world where there would be no fishes, pav bhaji, Ma, Papa. Or Auntyji. As if reading my thoughts, she brightened and said, "You are getting so much more Poonam, why do you want less?"

I kept looking back after security. Auntyji flanked by my mother and Usha Masi, kept smiling, waving. Ketaki, Papa, and Dinesh Uncle made another semi-circle. Soon everyone grew smaller and smaller and disappeared. Auntyji had the courage to do to the world what was never done to her. The new defeated Auntyji smiled with every cell of her body. Each time I went back home, it seemed like everything had changed. Everything except her smile -- a smile waiting for me after two years, after three, once after six. That smile maddened me. I wanted to shake her and ask her. *What are you so happy about Auntyji? What the fuck are you so happy about?*

Auntyji died last summer. I did get to see her one last time. Ma made me drive her all the way to the suburbs to Naveen's new place after he called us out of the blue, "Come quickly, she is awake today."

Ma ran to comb her hair and change her sari.

"But Ma, the driver is off today!"

Ma looked at me, her eyebrows only slightly raised.

"No, not in this traffic, I can't," I said.

But when we reached her home, she was asleep again.

"The meds are really unpredictable," Naveen was very apologetic. Barring the gray in his hair, he looked the same. Just a little stockier around the waist. I wondered how I appeared to him.

"Can we see her?" Naveen nodded. Ma and I took turns to peep through that open door. She didn't look sick. Her skin was still translucent, but there were heavy, dark circles under her eyes. I wanted to ask

Naveen; Does she smile still? Does she all the time?
But I didn't. It was an unusually cold Mumbai morning
when they cremated Auntyji. We took a soggy taxi to
the cremation ground. I didn't cry much all through but
when the rain filtered through the taxi windows, I cried
all I wanted to while Ma and Usha Masi squeezed each
hand. I did the same for them. So much had changed.
Auntyji was gone. Romi is almost where I once was.
Our city has a new name. It is also no longer my city. It
is old in new. I am old. So much had changed but then
we had changed nothing. When we got off the taxi, the
vermillion sari clad black haired doll strung to the taxi
mirror, continued spinning circles in and out. The rain
continued filtering through the windows. All we had
left behind was the smell of wet clothes on Rexene.

*

This mirror is meant to distort. They are funny
amusement mirrors. Yet today I am struck by my
purple heels and by how grotesque I look. On a day
that I have made determined effort to be otherwise.
They have given me their bags. I am holding on to
things not mine. Romi's pink clutch, one back pack,
one for each boy, I look down at my clingy green tights
and I wonder why I got into them. My cellphone is
blinking, it's Ketaki wanting to know. I think of the
countless long distance hours she has spent listening
to me over the last decade and I am suddenly
ashamed. Everything is moving in circles around me.
I see not what I should see but everything else – red
BEST buses, local Mumbai trains, graduate forms, the
blur of the labor room, Romila's wrinkled face, Eric's

shameless eyes, my single unpainted fingernail when Nick when will first find me, our hesitant kisses, a diamond ring on fingers not mine, my mocha colored nails, my expectant face, my voice, his voice and then Ketaki's from our last conversation.... *He is the one, Poonam, this time we will get lucky…..this time we will get lucky….*They are stopping the rides. The rain is getting heavier; they are walking towards me.

Romi looks disappointed, the boys, Terry and Jason too. I want to run to Romi and tell her … *There was ring, but not for me.* But no, *this i*s one secret I will never share with Romi. I turn my face. Cover my eyes with shades. Soon no one will be able to tell how my face actually got wet. Nick sits beside me. His body is taut. I can sense his tension, his fear at my hysteria spilling out on front of Romi and the boys. *Come out and say it.* I challenged him. He says nothing. He, who is normally flamboyant, unguarded, looks blank; this is his angry face. I wish I could borrow his face. I want to run to the ride operator and beg him, beg him with the money in my bank, beg him for one ride. In this rain-kissed air, I want to ride this roller coaster. I want it to take me to the highest point in the sky and fling these bags from that point. I want to look into the eyes of the sky from that point and say, and say, yes, yes, Auntyji, you were right. We have a waited a lifetime for luck. For love. In different countries. In apartments. In single family homes. On train stations. On roller coasters. We have lived in door open apartments, heart open; bodies, always expectant. Forgetting a lesson repeated; that whichever freeway you take this heart is going to break. Over and over offering ourselves to be fooled. Our degrees, our beauty, our midriff - baring saris, our cunning affording no protection. Many years ago I had said to Eric, "Why can only white girls get lost? In their search for a man who gives more than name and baby? No, not so. Give us a chance. We will prove to be equally competent." He stared at me, his fists shaking at some invisible demon, "Jesus Poonam! You are enough to drive any man crazy." I will not see him alone ever again after that moment. Today he is sane. No longer my Eric. My words have come true. I wanted so much for life to prove me a liar. But I am just crazy and true. Yes, Auntyji, Auntyji, You were right. Saab Jhoota hai. It's all a bloody lie.

Ants

Just 20 weeks into her first pregnancy and Gayatri already felt like a veteran. Pregnancy had turned out to be a lot like sex; messy, unpredictable and exhilarating. The exhilarating part came once every month when her ob-gyn would press a portable Doppler to her abdomen and make her listen to some *whoosh shoosh dub dub* sounds which she was told was her baby. The messy part, however, seemed omnipresent. Each moment brought with itself some additional proof of her present status as an incubator – whether it be the lumps in her armpits, her colossal breasts, the all pervading nausea, her sniffer dog nose, or her body's rejection of her favorite caffeine. But of course, she didn't dare complain. Not to her husband, Gautam, or mother or doctor. Not to anyone. Certainly never to herself.

Still, today had been harder than usual. It was barely noon and Gayatri had thrown up three times already. The last wave of nausea had culminated in her flushing down half-masticated remains of *idli sambhar,* soft white rice cakes eaten with a yellow lentil soup, her favorite south Indian fare. Half-dazed, Gayatri balanced herself on the flush tank and flushed the toilet one more time hoping that another rush of water would do something to lighten the unmistakable stench that wasenveloping the bathroom and increasingly the rest of the house, wondering simulatenously how she'd summon the will to conjure up another meal.

As a teenager with two plaits in Scared Heart Convent, New Delhi, Gayatri had viewed pregnancy as mostly a minor inconvenience to a woman's vanity, as an excuse for being pampered, for getting the latest clothes and accessories during the baby shower, the *Godh Bharai*. Her own pregnancy turned out to be quite a revelation - for despite having lived in one of the most populous countries in the world for twenty-four years, she had hardly ever encountered any pregnant woman up close. In her present pregnant status, she often found herself pondering why women should have to pay such a huge physical and mental price to be mothers. How could *nani,* her grandmother *have* brought herself to have six babies? Perhaps, she surmised, it had been the most natural thing to do at that time. This, retching, vomiting *alone* over toilet bowls, did not appear normal to Gayatri.

It had not been as natural for Gayatri. After a year and half of trying and countless tests, the only antidote her gynecologist had been able (or rather wanted) to prescribe, was to 'lighten up and stop thinking about it and if it still doesn't happen come back in six months'. So Gayatri took a leave of absence from her grueling job at a graphic design firm and became a freelance graphic designer. Gautam took her to Big Island and Victoria in quick succession. She shopped at Victoria's Secret and Walgreens and picked up generous doses of lingerie, lubricating jelly and St. John's Wort (*God forbid their families in India should know about it!*). Gayatri missed work. She missed her morning routine, the drive through coffee, the petty lunch time talk. Heck, she even missed her co-workers. But baby making took time. Diligence. And thus the Nandas, they ploughed on. Making time for frequent doctor visits. For yoga classes. For aqua aerobics. The Nandas also took time to view incredibly beautiful night skies, eat all types of cuisines, and have as little contact as possible with people in possession of drooling little infants. Six months went by and still nothing – Gayatri and Gautam braced themselves for the giant leap into the vast unknown of fertility treatments. Right after she had scheduled an appointment with a fertility specialist, a red-eyed Gayatri felt a strange tug in her womb and on a random instinct pulled out a stick from her medicine cabinet and peed on it. That day, four months ago, Gayatri's world changed forever. She had flushed her bathroom toilet countless times since then.

As she made her way to the kitchen to fetch her pregnancy staple of a glass of 2% Horizon milk, three slices of gently toasted Wonder bread and a small packet of Indian Glucose biscuits called Parle G, Gayatri thought about how this new blessing seemed to have eclipsed her almost inexplicable obsession with cleanliness and perfection. She, now, just did enough to get by and she was a little surprised that things hadn't fallen apart. An observation that didn't quite help her rise above her own guilt. "When the baby is a few months old," she said to Gautam, "we should do some major renovation, but right now..." Gayatri paused, caressing her slowly inflating tummy, her voice trailing of.

Despite her proclaimed negligence, when Gayatri caught a sedulous single file of ants making their way around the kitchen sink, she found herself scrubbing the kitchen countertop with a wet paper towel almost reflexively. Perhaps they had been attracted by the bread crumbs left behind by Gautam in his hurry to fix himself a sandwich for breakfast. But even this mild exertion tired her and she was relieved to be done with it and back on her bed. In the evening as he was folding their Nob Hill paper grocery bags, Gautam observed, "There are some ants near the fridge Gayatri."

"It's the height of summer – we need to be careful about leaving food crumbs around. I'll have Martha come by later in the week to do a deep clean." Martha came and went but the ants didn't go away.

Initially they would joke about it. "Do you know Gayatri," said Gautam, ever the store house of random information, "that a human brain has 10,000 million brain cells, so a colony of 40,000 ants has collectively the same size brain as a human!" Gayatri could offer only a feeble laugh in response. Working from home with all its inbuilt distractions had not been easy and now with the ants around it was becoming close to impossible. She had nearly missed a deadline earlier in the day because she had spent a major part of her morning playing Hitler to a short lived ant holocaust. It was almost as if the more ferocity with which Gayatri scrubbed, the more vengeance with which the ants returned.

Days passed and Gayatri became more disgruntled. Having been hardwired into believing that pregnancy would be her time for rest and relaxation, it seemed unfair to her to have to work this fruitlessly hard. Gayatri longed for the public displays of affection that would have been hers had they chosen to birth their child in India, oblivious to the secret preparations for her upcoming baby shower. An American baby shower, but a shower nonetheless. A baby shower in which people would give them things for the unborn little one, a sure invitation to bad luck in the eyes of her *nani* ("*Who buys things for the unborn*?"). A shower in which Gautam's friends would plaster the rented walls of the community room in a nearby apartment complex with PartyCity bought supplies and scream "Surprise!" as she would enter wearing the last of her *Banarasi* saris that did not need dry cleaning, self-consciously tugging at her four-year-old stretch blouse covered under a delicately embroidered Kashmiri shawl. A shower in which she would cut a sickeningly sweet cake with layers and layers of cream decorated with tiny little pink bootees slung from the beak of a tired looking white bird. But that was many, many weekends away. Before that they would have to reclaim their lives from the ants. For now, each day became a quagmire of meaningless events. With each passing day the ants became bolder and bolder. They crawled over shins, into a sleeping Gautam's ears and on their unsuspecting laundry. Soon the ants had begun to vie with their unborn for conversation space. From being an obsessive compulsive pregnancy bulletin board reader Gayatri became an obsessive ant remedy junkie.

"Someone at work suggested that we vacuum the ants as soon as we see them," said Gautam one evening. Gayatri kept silent; she had already tried that. Each time she moved the vacuum it would excite fearful contractions in her uterus and she would be forced to abandon the project right away. By another week Gayatri had begun to live in fear, forgetting to celebrate the fact that her nausea had faded away. When she would finish windexing *them* on the kitchen hardwood, she found *them* taking over the living room. Slowly the ants made way onto the staircase carpet and into their bathrooms. Gautam chipped in whenever he could, vacuuming and spraying but for the most part he was away at work, which meant that Gayatri fought her battle alone. Meanwhile, the baby's kicks had become stronger and more predictable and the doctor beamingly announced that Gayatri was carrying a girl child. Gautam got busy putting together a shortlist of names; Gayatri promptly choose *Jaya,* meaning victory in Sanskrit. But this heady anticipation was adulterated with desperation – how would they welcome their newborn in an ant infested home? Almost all their friends and acquaintances volunteered possible causes and remedies.

"Maybe they are coming into the house because it's so hot outside," said Rudy, the UPS guy.

"Maybe they're hungry," said Gayatri's cousin caught in traffic on Highway 101N, following that up with an offbeat spiritual solution, "Put some rice and sugar in plate in the garden and pray to the ants to go away."

Maybe you need to clean the garden and the garage storage. Something's inviting them - caulk everything. Maybe, Maybe. Then the solutions – find where they are coming from and **try** …. puffs of baby powder, vinegar, boric acid powder, red chili powder, turmeric, bay leaves, cinnamon, coffee, ant killer granules and more. Most advice was offered with confidence but an equal amount came with a why-don't–you-try-it-you-have-nothing-to-lose look. But what everyone seemed to be in agreement upon was that fact that the ants needed to go away. The question was always how, never why.

In a few days red chili powder, coffee, bay leaves and many others had all paid their dues but the ants would still not go away. The only antidotes that seemed to work temporarily were vinegar and Vaseline. As she spread Vaseline on the countertop Gayatri thought of all the prenatal massages her mother would have arranged for her had she chosen to deliver her baby at her parents' home. Another immigrant penalty - and Gayatri made no attempt to reason with an anger that was rapidly raising its head. Why bother keeping it, when there was no one around to admonish her for losing it? Five minutes later, all the unfolded laundry found itself dispossessed and tentative, crouching in different corners of the living room and the kitchen.

The steel cutlery would have been next in line had her unborn not stepped in and pressed the pause button by giving Gayatri a firm and kicking reminder of exigent reality.

"Just call the pest controlwala *beta*," said the *desi* grocery store owner finally.

"No ji" said his wife from behind the DVD racks, "It's not good for the baby. Just be patient *beta,* they'll go away. How long can they stay?" she said cheerfully. *Long enough for me to lose my sanity,* thought Gayatri. Eventually one Saturday morning when Gayatri woke up to find her dream home scrawled with red-brown lines and smelling of vinegar and petroleum jelly, she decided to that they needed to call the pest control. "Are you sure?" asked Gautam tentatively. Gayatri nodded.

"I'll look for a pest control company later this afternoon," Gautam stroked Gayatri's cheek with his index finger, "But before that why don't we take a warm scented bath and follow it up with a leisurely breakfast?"

Gayatri lumbered to the bath tub and filled it with water. She took lots of baths nowadays. She felt lighter, safer, and cleaner in the water. In the afternoon when Gautam thought that Gayatri was safely asleep he made a call to the closest pest control company he had found on Yahoo! local. He didn't bother to step away from the bedroom to make the call, for Gayatri was an incredibly deep sleeper, forgetting however that pregnancy had changed many things about her.

"Hello! All-in-One Exterminator, How may I help you?" Gautam paused. The voice seemed perfect, was this an answering machine or a real human?

"*Hellloooo?*"

"Yes, Hello. This is Gautam Nanda. I live in Fremont. I was looking to have some pest control done in my house."

"What do you have?" the woman asked.

"Ants."

The mere mention of the word *ant* roused Gayatri's from her light sleep, but she still kept her eyes closed and pretended to be resting.

"Spiders, bugs, termites, anything else?"

"No, nothing."

"Well, if you have ants, the chances are pretty high that you'll have some kind of termites too," said the operator matter of factly.

Gautam cringed. "I hope not."

"Well, you really can't see them. What kind of ants do you have – red, white, black?"

"Black ants," said Gautam. Gayatri shifted her clenched fist to cover her eyes and shuddered at the thought of the vast ocean of ants that would be awaiting them when they went downstairs.

"Hmm, so here's what we offer..." said the pest control lady. Gayatri could hear some faint typing in the background.

Gautam interrupted the operator, "My wife is pregnant and in her second trimester. Will what you do be safe for the baby?" There was a brief pause and whatever the sales woman at the other end said was not particularly audible. Now Gautam spoke again, "Oh how wonderful! Congratulations on your pregnancy. It's comforting to know that you had pest control done at your place last week as well."

That doesn't mean anything. We don't know anything till the baby is delivered. Gayatri felt her chest tighten with rage. Was that marketing at its zenith or just her inability to absorb a compassionate reassurance.

"Alright then, how about having someone take care of it early next week?" said Gautam.

"How about this coming Monday?" said the pest control lady.

"Sure," replied Gautam and kept the receiver down.

Gayatri was now sitting up. "Heyhoney. You're up! I spoke to the..."

"I know, I heard," replied Gayatri sullenly.

The Nandas spent Sunday with close friends, and for a little while the ants were relegated into the background.

"Gautam I was..." said Gayatri as they drove back. A significant majority of their profound conversations about life, career, childbirth, took place in the car.

"I don't think we need to cancel Gayatri. The baby's going to be fine," Gautam preempted her.

"Well then, here's what I feel - let's just surrender to them and welcome them in our home," said Gayatri. Gautam kept his eyes on the steering wheel. He knew there was no reasoning with his wife now.

"If we have to take care of them ourselves, then we must set some ground rules. Seal everything. Put everything in boxes. And we are going to eat out everyday," said Gautam.

"For how long?" asked Gayatri.

"However long it takes," said Gautam, "And…. you will now work out of the library or Starbucks, and will do no more than one round of vinegar mopping and Vaseline…"

"I need the comfort of home. I need to go to the bathroom frequently, to throw up and to…" Gayatri protested.

"You'll get used it. If not anything, these ants will teach us how to be persistent," said Gautam firmly.

Finally surrendering to sharing the roof with the hardest working creatures in this world seemed to do the trick, or at least partly. Each morning Gayatri would get up, make a cup of tea for Gautam, ("You don't need to do that," he had said to her in the early months of her pregnancy. "I want to," she replied. "This way I can smell the enticing aroma of tea.") pour herself some milk and cereal and then soak an old hand towel in a generous mixture of part vinegar and part water and mop the kitchen floor. This routine would be followed by a light Vaseline scrub on the countertop.

Days passed and Gayatri almost felt like herself again. Her seventh month had started and during the ultrasound the doctor told them that the baby looked "terrific". The seventh was a special month. A time when the baby could hear well, be active and still not feel extremely confined in the womb, while the mother continued to enjoy the benefits of the second trimester. Now was time to enroll in childbirth classes and to get ready for the countdown. Gautam finally agreed to Gayatri's choice of baby name. Continents away Gayatri's mother got her visa from the American embassy and booked her ticket to SFO. The summer made way for fall and the ants looked spent after fighting valiantly against Vaseline, coffee, vinegar, chili powder, turmeric and many such enemies.

Three weeks before the baby was due, the kitchen countertops were much cleaner and the house was almost spotless. The cleaners came often and Gautam had become very efficient at vacuuming ants anywhere he saw them in the house. After a month's reprieve the Nandas had slowly started cooking again and a home cooked meal awaited Gayatri's mother who was due to arrive later in the day. Still Gayatri found it hard to let go of her habit of putting generous amounts of Vaseline on the kitchen countertop.

"Gayatri! We're getting late for the airport," Gautam called out from the garage.

"Hang on, I need some water." As Gayatri was pouring herself some water she saw a tiny black baby ant struggling against the vast Vaseline covered white ceramic tiled landscape of the kitchen countertop. A miniscule baby ant with fine antennae, shoving its tiny appendages doggedly through the sticky gunk of the petroleum jelly. Suddenly Gayatri felt a wave of tenderness towards this ant. She opened her kitchen dresser and pulled out a blunt knife and set it in front of this baby ant. The ant touched the knife drunkenly and got onto it. Three hours later Gayatri showed off her spotless countertop to her mother. The baby ant was gone.

The Ragpicker

Aparita saw the ragpicker every day. On days that she was on time, that is. Whenever Rohan took longer to eat his cereal or his carpool friend Monica made them wait outside because she couldn't decide on the colour of the beads that would go on her braids; she would slip. Aparita would feel a deep reassurance and pity whenever she saw her. Pity because not unlike other things, poverty was lonely too in America. Aparita knew that they did not speak the same language.

Jing, the ragpicker, worked alone. First she circled the apartment complex. After that she searched the dumpster near the strip mall, the one next to the Hair and Nails. Then she liked to do something unpredictable. Like sip on the last of her Treetop apple juice cans that the brown woman had once brought her. Jing felt such pity for her whenever she tried; broken Mandarin, gesticulating fingers. Other days Jing would park her cart near the dumpster and go sit on one of the park benches and look at birds flying in the sky.

Aparita made a conscious decision not to reprimand Rohan even though he routinely woke up late all summer. She knew he would never have a childhood like hers. The least she could offer him was one summer. Then one cool, bright evening while Rohan was waiting for her impatiently in front of Cold Stone Creamery, Aparita made a U-turn at the traffic light and chased the nimble-footed hunch back of her neighborhood. She gesticulated to the old woman to wait – thrust her right hand forward, pulled it back, pushed it out against the air, back again. The old woman nodded. Aparita took a deep breath, grinned lopsidedly like she once had when someone she had watched from the corners of her eyes had returned that glance and not unlovingly at that. She drove back home, threw a carton of Costco Treetop in her trunk. Some water too.

Jing has found a friend. He is 30 years her junior and calls her "old sister". Together they criss-cross the train tracks and circle the supermarkets. Jing goes East. He goes North. They work an extra hour each day. They know it'll be hard to rummage during dark, winter nights.

Aparita felt jealous the first time she saw him. Then happy. Then jealous. Then happy again. She was never curious. The old woman continues to wear the same clothes. Black pants, faded black full sleeves, a loose baggy muddy tunic on top of it all. A red and black checkered scarf. It's hard to tell if the scarf might have been silk once.

She flicked her hand back and then waved it from left to right. Twice. Aparita knew that they did not speak the same language so she thrust (another time), the white packet stuffed with the maroon blanket embroidered with yellow daisies in front of the old woman's creased face. Aparita suddenly realized that the woman was almost as tall as Rohan. "For you," she said. *For you. These juice cans. For you.* In Mandarin. In English. In another unnecessary language. Jing flicked her hand and said something Aparita did not understand. Aparita parted her lips wide to expose her teeth. It was not a smile because it never reached her eyes. The older woman nodded, adjusted her head scarf and pushed her cart ahead. Aparita thought she saw the old woman's wrinkles reach beyond her eyes, almost to her forehead, even though she had never parted her lips. She knew that the old woman had smiled. Aparita sees her everyday. She no longer feels pity for her. Sometimes the earth is not thirsty. When Aparita looks towards the sky, she can now imagine the gratitude of a cloud that has been allowed to burst.

Near Death Experience

When he fell, Dev felt a brief lift and then a drop. The air had the same moist and fragrant quality that surrounded his mother on Sundays when after oiling her hair, she would take a head bath and then neglect to dry her hair - busying herself instead, thin handloom towel wrapped around her tresses, with frying, peeling, grating, chopping, smiling. The air was crisp and soft, like the wisps of cotton that flew out his and his brother Mohit's pillows when they'd hit each other. His eyes were closed. Dev heard Ma say, *we'll come to the moon for you*. Everything was fresh. Almost beautiful.

*

It had been many years since Dev had wondered about what to do next. From the moment he'd arrived at O'Hare airport with two suitcases and five hundred dollars, Dev knew what his short term goals were. The first to get his Masters degree. The second to get away from the blistering Chicago cold. He accomplished both in 18 months. He took the first job he was offered, not because he was afraid that he would not find another, but because he always trusted his first instinct. And his instinct told him to go to California.

Dev made friends with Viren on the first day of work soon after they found out that they had a birth city in common. Viren lived close, he had steady roommates. Dev didn't have much luck with roommates and lived by himself in a one-bedroom apartment. Within six months, Dev and Viren had decided to share the rent for a two bedroom. They carpooled to work sometimes but often Dev would be up really early and so he went by himself. They continued as roommates even after Viren switched jobs a few months later.

Soon Dev and Viren settled into an easy, uncomplicated camaraderie that only men can share. They played tennis on Saturday mornings. On occasional Sundays they rounded up all their classmates from their respective Indian alma maters and hobbled together a cricket team that loved cricket enough to play it on a baseball field with sticks bought from OSH as stumps, and, of course, the tennis ball. Sometimes they would rent movies from the neighborhood movie stores. More often than not, the DVDs would lie unopened on top of their second-hand oak coloured entertainment center, awaiting their return to home base, but not before their mere presence had pilfered Dev and Viren of some late fees.

One summer Viren went to India and returned two months later with Mrs. Narang. His wife. Smita was a petite, dusky programmer who arrived on American shores with an offer letter from Nokia in her pocket.

Viren's friends and co-workers threw Smita a welcome party. Dev wore a shirt from Gap and a pair of jeans from Guess accessorized with a watch Viren had carried over the seas; a gift from Dev's mother. All the women in the party teased Dev about being the most eligible bachelor in their circle. Dev felt compelled to tell them that they were basing their observations on a very small sample size. "*Anything* will look good to you after your husbands," he said. He was not joking.

While Dev was happy for Viren, he could not place the reason for his faint discomfort each time he glanced at Smita. Three weeks after Viren and Smita's Silicon Valley wedding reception, Dev got his green card. This time Viren and Smita took Dev out for a celebration. Over dinner, Dev zeroed-in on the fact that Smita's mannerisms reminded him of Masuko and he immediately relaxed.

Dev had been wondering what to do with himself ever since he had been forced to say goodbye to his comfortable job at Uber Graphics three months ago. Division restructuring was what they called it. The company had been generous to him. Since he was one of the initial employees of what had once been a start-up, they gave him an almost unprecedented, six-month severance. Dev took it well. Not personally. It had nothing to do with his abilities. Viren told him it was a blessing in disguise. The day after his lay off, it hit him that he hadn't seen his parents for over a year now and the only friend he had made in his seven years in America was Viren. He hadn't done badly, but he could have done better. What could have been better? Not having his father tell him two years and nine months ago, that, the name of the friendly Japanese librarian was Masuko. For sure. Dev was not sure about anything else.

During his break, Dev read PoBronson's *What Should I Do With My Life* and Nelson Mandela's autobiography. He decided to make a three week India trip and booked his tickets with a travel agent for a tentative date. He was sure he wanted to be employed before he saw his parents, though. He also took long walks, slept late, ate out some and cooked at home some. He was astonished at the amount of cleaning one had to do after even the simplest meal and decided to enlist the services of a cleaner for his small, modest apartment. On weekends, he went to the community library, checked out books and gazed at a girl with a petite frame and shiny black hair, from a distance. Sometimes he came face to face with Masuko and they exchanged *hellos.* The days Masuko wore her paisley skirts with white tops and her hair down were the days he liked best. Of late, Masuko had started offering specific book recommendations. The last one happened to be a book from her personal bookshelf, her name and email at the top right side of page one.

At the beginning of the fourth month of his forced holiday, Dev tried to give some gas to his friendship with Viren which had been on cruise control ever since Viren had gotten married. They met at a neighborhood Indian restaurant famed for its spicy North Indian buffets.

"Any luck with the job hunt?" Viren asked spooning some dal onto his rice from the buffet table.

"Nah yaar, not very much. I want to do something different this time. I want to feel the juice."

"You should talk to my friend Chitresh. He's starting a new company and they've got two million in seed money. He's always had his eye on you."

"Will do. Two million in seed money. Wow!"

By now they were at their assigned table with the server bringing them naans. The naans were soft and piping hot. Dev liked how they felt inside the hollow of his mouth but not what they did to his stomach afterwards. Or maybe it was the sabzi peppered with tangy aamchur that was to blame.

"I think the juice is there for people who are focused," said Viren. "And the focus comes from the destination. But I am not sure what the destination is anymore."

And just then Dev had a longing for those cold, wintry days spent plowing through the slowness of the snow. He felt a longing to touch-wear his first shirt bargain-bought from his meager assistant stipend. Then he remembered that he didn't like the cold, the way it made the fingers feel like they didn't belong on your body.

"Do you remember Cooper, our first boss at Uber?" asked Viren.

Dev nodded.

"I think he was one of the most focused people I've met in my life. So efficient with his time."

"He was," Dev agreed.

"I wonder how he got there."

Dev knew. Cooper had been mauled in a horrific road accident as a teenager. It took him three years to fully recover.

"I wouldn't have said it then, but that accident made me, *me,*" Cooper had told Dev during a private conversation one evening as they were both working late.

"Once you look at your worst fear in the eye, there is nothing to be afraid of anymore. After *that,* I figured, a little time is all I've got," he'd said.

Dev retired early that evening but couldn't sleep. He emailed Chitresh his resume and heard back from him within an hour. Chitresh was in South Korea; he promised to meet Dev as soon as he got back.

Dev warmed himself a cup of milk and sat down to watch TV. He ruminated over his afternoon conversation with Viren. He doodled on a notepad. Wrote stray thoughts. *Path to changeà Confront a fear.* Dev didn't have too many fears that had persisted to adulthood – losing Ma and Papa. Yeah, that was a biggie. Poverty. Not anymore. Wealth came from skills, from attention, not inheritance. America had put paid to that one. Marrying a girl who was not his parents' choice. Not really. He knew they'd come around - in two hours, maximum two days. *Then why so long*? A little voice inside him asked. "I am no longer a devotee of Newton's first law of motion. I will remedy this immediately," Dev said to himself and flung one of the futon's taupe cushions in the air as celebration. Next he found Masuko's book. Started and saved an email draft. He would eventually complete the email and press *Send* after he'd read 15 pages of the Masuko-recommended, Masuko-owned, *The Death of Ivan Ilyich.*

It was getting late at night. Dev continued ruminating. Roller coasters. Height. Circles. The memories came to him in snapshots, each one folding into the other seamlessly. Ten-year-old Dev vomiting in Ma's lap in their little Ferris wheel boogie. The discomfort of the long lines at the Empire State Building only magnified by the dizziness and nausea he felt at the top. The abandoned journey to the Half Dome. How might all those memories be redeemed? Perhaps a rollercoaster ride? *Nah.* Dev flipped a channel. Perhaps a trip to the Empire State again? *Too Easy.* Flip to another channel. A bunch of amateur ecstatic skydivers. Ecstatic, safe, glorious. Full of love and reverence. For life. For the world. *That was it.*

The next morning, in his typical fashion, Dev spent a lot of time researching his decision. But he knew that he had already made his choice. Everything else was window dressing.

"The instructor is highly trained; I suppose?" asked Dev. The chirpy voice at the other end of the phone replied with a lilt in her voice, "John's the best. He has over 5000 tandem jumps to his credit and over 7000 accelerated ones." A couple of other questions and it was settled.

"How would you like to pay?" she asked.

"Next Friday then!" she said cheerily as they hung up.

Everything changed for Dev the moment his gave the operator his credit card number. He made himself a cup of tea and called his parents. His standard once a week call. He told them nothing about how he had spent his morning. Then he went out for a run.

The last time Dev was anywhere near roller coasters was when Ma and Papa came visiting. Three years ago, father retired from his position as General Manager of the State Bank, the same year Mohit started college in Kanpur.

"When will you come Papa, if not now?" Dev asked. Reluctantly his father applied for a visa and in a few weeks they boarded a flight to SFO via Hong Kong. When Dev saw his father at the airport he was shocked at how much he seemed to have aged in the past 18 months since Dev's last trip home.

"Ma, has Papa stopped eating?"

Ma just smiled and said, "Just what happens to Fathers *beta,* as their sons become men."

Ma settled into a routine faster than Papa. She busied herself cooking and cleaning in the apartment. Pa took a little longer, but the public library system was a big solace. On weekdays, Dev would rush home after work to spend as much time as possible with Ma and Papa. On weekends, he would take them city seeing around the Bay Area. The first two weekends, Dev's parents sampled the sights of San Francisco.

One evening when he might have typically worked late, Dev forced himself to wrap up things sooner and come home. When Dev got to the apartment he saw that his mother was busy getting the dough ready for rotis and his father was sitting on the single most comfortable piece of furniture, the reclining leather chair and reading *The Wall Street Journal*. *The New York Times* and *The San Francisco Chronicle* had possibly made their entry and exit earlier in the day. America had reduced his parents to overgrown children in forcible house arrest.

"I am so sorry Papa, the public transport connections are not very good in this area."

His father looked up from his newspaper, half-smiled and asked rhetorically, "Par hamhe kahan jaana hai? *Where do we need to go?*"

Ma came toward Dev with a plateful of snacks and sat him down on the table, cupped his chin and a little bit of his cheek and said, "Don't worry about us *beta*. You are our home. We'll come to the moon for you." Overcome Dev hugged Ma while Papa continued to read his newspaper, the car lobby now forgiven.

It was Papa who struck a friendship with Masuko, the library assistant who would be soon promoted to librarian, and allowed Dev to get his foot in the door of Masuko's consciousness.

"Nice girl, that Japanese assistant," Papa would tell Ma approvingly, "she's very sharp and recommends good books." Ma would sigh heavily and wave her rolling pin in the air, "Books, books...always books!"

When they went out, Papa and Dev took turns taking photographs. So it was Dev and Ma in a red-beige sari in front of Nordstrom at the Valley Fair Mall. Papa and Dev in Yosemite. But the vineyards captivated all three of them so deeply that they just *had* to ask more than one stranger to take family photographs. Dev drank wine, white more often than red, but he didn't drink any when he took his parents on a wine tour to Napa. Papa gave Dev the green signal many times in different ways, like when he said, *when in Rome, do as Romans my father would say Dev,* but Dev didn't feel the need. He felt fortunate just soaking in the familiar, the much loved, with the newly discovered.

The week preceding his skydive, everything appeared changed to Dev. He didn't hate the dowdy furniture in his apartment as much. He made his bed soon after he woke up. He lingered longer while shaving and shaved cleaner. He glanced at the picture of Ma, Papa and himself in Napa many times during the day and smiled frequently. He ran with the wind kissing his face in circles on the green grass, not on the hard, knee cracking concrete. He didn't inch his car slowly towards pedestrians. He emailed Masuko for a date. They would meet Saturday. For lunch. Then a movie, perhaps? *Will you wear your hair down*? He asked her. She wrote back. *Yes. Anything else?*

Dev called his parents on Wednesday.

"I miss you so much Ma," he said suddenly.

There was silence at the other end. He knew his mother was negotiating a lump in her throat. He went on, "When you see me the next time Ma, you'll be so proud of me. I am going to be a new person."

"I am proud of you *now*, Dev," was all Ma could say, half-laughing, half-crying.

Thursday night Viren came to visit. Smita was away on an offsite and Viren could no longer tolerate the feel of an empty home. It was getting late. An infomercial kept them company in the background.

"I'm having Smita take them," said Viren.

"What?"

Viren made two small circles with his forefinger and thumb and placed those circles equidistant on his ribcage.

"What! Breasts what?

"Enhancers," said Viren.

"Wow," said Dev.

"Yeah..." said Viren tightening a little.

"Can you even increase their size?" said Dev.

Viren nodded confidently. "It's just fat after all. That's what the infomercial said."

"Saala... you're crazy!"

"Not as crazy as you. Scared of heights and going sky diving," Viren replied quietly, his arms folded across his chest.

"Who's to decide?" said Dev gaily.

Viren got up to leave. His eyes caught an airmail envelope from India lying on top of Dev's Craigslist community listing scoured TV.

"How did you like the pictures? Are you bringing Smita a friend soon?" Viren said, lightening up a little.

"Oh...not bad, not bad," said Dev colouring a bit. "But...." he hesitated. "Do you remember Masuko?" Viren looked at Dev blankly for just a moment.

"Library lady?"

Dev smiled. "I asked her out, finally!"

"Saala, who's the chupa rustom here?" asked Viren, rhetorically

Dev had a hard time getting sleep that night. He dreamt of Masuko both before and after going to sleep. He would take Masuko to the neighborhood summer carnival soon. They would sit on the carousel and eat ice cream. Strawberry for her, chocolate for him. They would go round and round. Round and round on horses and in little Ferris wheel boogies. Then he'd boldly slide his hand over hers. But he would go no further. At least in that moment. Dev awoke close to dawn with a deep, deep longing to call Masuko. It was too early, so he wrote her an email. *You are... I am... You are...* The words did not fail him; they lined up rapidly in front of each other, not with the precision of soldiers but with the innocence of little children beckoned by a teacher to stand in file.

*

Everything went as planned. The waiting. The putting-on of preparatory gear. The most wonderful John. The ride in the airplane. The strapping morphing John and Dev into Siamese twins. The readying to jump from 12,500 feet.

"Now," said John and now it was. The jump a medley of slow motion and supersonic speed. Dev felt that the sky looked even more beautiful than it did to him before his flights from India would touch down at SFO. And Dev kept falling, falling.

The TV crews came swarming, (it had been a dull week otherwise) not too long after the emergency personnel. John was sitting by a tree, wrapped in a blanket, trying not to cry.

--Did he look frightened to you?

--- No. He was a picture of calm.

--- Was he alive during the free fall?

--- Yes.

--- When did you know he had gone?

-- After I pulled the parachute and the descent started. He was not responding.

-- What did he say to you during the free fall?

-- He said, it's incredible. I said, *welcome to my world*. He laughed. A minute later he said... I feel like a new person.

Up in the sky, the airplanes shared the sky with the birds. It was the loveliest day.

Daddy Cool

America had made Goverdhan into Gov within two months of arrival. But Goverdhan never complained. "I am lucky," he would joke to his Indian friends decades later, "that people call me Gov without having to run for office." For three decades Goverdhan had paid America the ultimate compliment by electing to stay in a country that did not birth him. Today, America decided to return the compliment. As Goverdhan took the Highway 237 to his home, he could not stop breaking into involuntary smiles every few seconds. The Mayor's words reverberated in his ears, *Gov Yadav is not just a fine entrepreneur, he epitomizes the spirit of innovation that has made America the pride of the world.* The Mayor's voice alternated with his dead grandfather's baritone. *A new school for the village, jobs for extended family, who would have thought a cow herd's grandson capable of all this. No one, except me.*

A stray tear rolled down Goverdhan's cheek and he said softly, "Who else but you, *dadaji* who else?" The fragrance emanating from the rose bouquet on the passenger seat of his Mercedes brought Goverdhan back to the present moment briefly and he changed lanes. But it was hard not to relive the events of the day – the exciting energy of the Convention Hall, the admiring glances of colleagues from the community. On his way out a young man with an accent similar to his had asked him eagerly, "Goverdhan *ji* what is the secret of your success?" Goverdhan smiled beatifically and said, "Just understand the system *bhai*□. Just that. America rewards those who understand its systems."

Five minutes away from home, his cell phone rang.

"*Kahan ho*? Where are you?" It was Nalini.

"I am almost home," Goverdhan replied animatedly. "I've had the most amazing day, can't wait to tell you."

As he pulled his car into the driveway, Goverdhan's heart pounded like it wanted out from its cage. Where *were* his two boys? Arun and Varun. Or Ahhroon and Vaaharoon as their kindergarten teacher Ms Trudy (and subsequently most of America) had christened them. He rushed right in, wanting to take them both by the scruffs of their necks and crush them close to his chest. Wanting to tell them that fifteen hours had been too long to go without seeing them, never mind the honors of the day. But once inside his house he stood dazed and unsettled as he encountered Mr. Lane and his thirteen-year-old son Daniel, who also happened to be Arun's best friend, sitting comfortably on the Yadav's plush marmalade and coffee sateen upholstered couch.

"Ah Gov. We missed you," said Mr. Lane cheerily, "We were talking about how much fun we had skiing last winter." Goverdhan grinned absentmindedly at Arun, his body suddenly tense. "Oh, I didn't know we had company," he said. Arun blushed, transforming himself into a paler, thinner, younger and more Americanized version of his father. At which Nalini crinkled her nose just a little, her eyes darting between father and son before fixing them on Goverdhan. "Chai?" she asked. Goverdhan nodded and Nalini excused herself to her kitchen.

"Mr. Lane, our last meeting was rather brief," said Goverdhan, trying to lighten the atmosphere. "I'd love to learn more about you. Arun tells me that you tried out for the Olympics once."

"Mr. Lane's a fabulous skier and a great athlete," said Arun, the adulation transparent in his eyes.

"Nah! It's no big deal. I bet you and Daniel will outshine me in a few seasons." At that, Varun sitting on the arm of the love seat next to Daniel coughed a small cough.

"That goes for you as well Varun," laughed Mr. Lane, his large frame shaking just a little. And then he looked at Goverdhan and with a conspiratorial look said, "We'll just add another two years to our estimate for Arun and Daniel!" Goverdhan half-smiled and shifted uneasily in his seat while fiddling with the rings on his pointer and ring fingers.

"We must get going now," Mr. Lane looked at Daniel, "It was great to have you boys with us last season. But this season I want to extend all of you an invitation to join us at Heavenly. We have a cottage all to ourselves and I am sure it'll be a lot of fun."

"Oh but Dad doesn't ski," said Arun.

"Dad's learning," interjected Varun.

The boys spoke with a self assurance that had taken Goverdhan three decades to accumulate.

"On the bunny slope?" asked Arun his brows arched, his voice sharp. Mr. Lane took a deep breath, "Well, you know what they say boys, it's never too late to learn."

Nalini returned with Goverdhan's chai.

"Nalini, I am so glad to have finally met you. Varun tells me that you make the most delectable samosas," said Mr. Lane.

"Perhaps when Mrs. Lane comes back from her conference, we can get together for high tea," said Nalini.

In the driveway, Mr. Lane rolled down his BMW windows and said, "I sure hope all of you can make it to Heavenly. The ladies can bond over massages and shopping while *we* men get our bones warm." Then in true swashbuckling style, he zoomed off as smoothly as he had arrived.

*

At night Goverdhan reclined against the bed frame of their California King bed reading under the illumination of a tiny book light, thinking Nalini to be asleep. Abruptly, Nalini turned around to face him and said, "It's alright. He's just a boy."

"I was such a different kind of a boy," Goverdhan said quietly, his balding forehead shining in the reflected light. Goverdhan felt a sudden longing for a childhood spent cleaning windows in dining cars, washing and milking cows. There was order in that universe.

"We lived in a different world then," said Nalini before going back to sleep.

Except on Diwali Goverdhan very rarely missed India. He had no time for it. For every few years, America presented him a mountain to climb; something he did with relish. But that his newest and fuzziest challenge should present itself so soon after his last success stunned Goverdhan. Or perhaps, could it be possible, that this was *not* a new problem? Perhaps this volcano had become active from the moment his Arun had set foot in the world 13 years ago and had been lurking in the background all the while his preschoolers laughed their effervescent giggles. Lurking while he told them the same story with a different cinematic flourish each time, their puppy eyes shining with pride.... *The climatic moment of my life was at the beginning of my 19th year....* Then suddenly, everything changed a few summers ago. Stories were not enough anymore. Unlike his *Babuji* who could do no wrong, his boys, especially Arun, measured Goverdhan's worthiness in tangible terms. *New clothes every semester* check, *dependable Dad* check, *no Ivy League* cross, *no hiking, fishing, playing tennis and swimming possible with father,* cross, cross, cross, cross. With each year he could feel that gulf becoming wider, its trenches deeper. How could he explain to his boys, whom he had failed by not giving them any empty spaces necessary in their life for gratitude, that he had never had any time in life to learn anything, save for how to live?

The following afternoon Goverdhan scarcely worked on the redesign of the motel that until yesterday had consumed most of his waking thoughts. He spent the first part of his lunch hour gazing at a picture of the three people who made his world. Nalini: Loyal and choiceless, except for the solitary choice of happiness that she had made and decided never to go back upon. Arun: The boy who held his tongue at school and carried his father's burden of assimilation on his shoulders. Varun: the third man in line, his shoulders resting easy under the protection of an older brother and the affluence of his father. He opened his desk drawer and pulled out a yellow notepad from a stack he had bought at *Costco* and made a small list. The questions that pushed him in directions that brought him to America returned again. *How do I project myself? How do I become the person who makes my family proud?*

It was list of things he knew his boys liked to do; he struck off some items from that list. Then he looked at his work schedule and made some calculations. In the end Goverdhan left himself with a three-item bulleted list - gym, tennis and swimming. At night he shared his decision with Nalini and when he saw the unspoken questions in her eyes said, "My Babuji did so many things for us, why can't I be a little stronger physically for my boys?"

The next day Goverdhan cut work to attend to more pressing matters. First, he enrolled himself in the neighborhood gym, then he signed himself up for an adult tennis class at the community center and finally, found himself an indoor heated pool that offered adult lessons as well as flexible practice hours. Goverdhan smiled inwardly with anticipation; every experience in the new world had taught him the meaning of an old word *afresh*. Which meaning would revise itself this time?

Now Goverdhan woke each morning at the crack of dawn, showered, did his morning *puja* and breathing exercises and went to the gym. There he spent forty minutes on the treadmill and twenty minutes on the stationary bike. One morning he met a young man who seemed strangely familiar. Then he remembered that his face was plastered right next to the stationary bike captioned *How I lost 45 pounds in 11 months*; 20 minutes everyday in front of the "Before" and "After" picture of this young man emboldened Goverdhan sufficiently that he could assume an air of intimate formality with him.

"I spend two hours in the gym everyday," said Goverdhan matter-of-factly.

"That's great man, but I think a trainer is the way to go," said the highly-toned and newly-improved Mr. After.

Goverdhan pondered that advice for over a week and when even after three weeks the scales refuse to budge towards his left, decided that $80 for an hour didn't sound like such a bad deal after all.

The trainer was a ruddy faced, affectionate man. He took one look at Goverdhan's 42-inch waist and insisted that besides his customized stamina building routine Goverdhan start with dynamic yoga classes as well. Dynamic yoga turned out to be a bastardized version of the original yogic movements, designed to combine the benefits of high level aerobic activity with the strength of yoga. Goverdhan was nothing if not an obedient student. He showed up twice a week and on time with his purple yoga mat. Within ten minutes he would be sweating voluminously and dizzy in the head. People nodded and smiled in sympathy when Goverdhan would have to step in a corner, sit, drink water and catch his breath. Some newcomers who might have otherwise rolled off the edges, stuck on because they were inspired by his example, by his repeated standing up after falling down, like an infant learning to walk. These classes made Goverdhan feel like what he had felt when he had first tried to read the BART timetables. But he continued to work with the single minded devotion that America had unlocked inside him. *Bhakta.* He had once learnt what a bhakta was. It fell somewhere between the gentle thuds of the BART that took him to his evening MBA classes and the meticulousness with which he served his customers at the restaurant. Bhakta. Devotee. Once America had taught him that it was not important to have, it was important to want and that wanting would pave the way for larger, more wondrous things. Now he would learn it again. He thought.

Early evenings, the labor of his mornings was replaced by P+P = P (Position + Preparation = Point) with Coach Barry at the Community Center Tennis Courts. The Coach never asked Goverdhan the question. A question, he was pretty sure, that was lingering on the tip of the Coach's tongue. *Why now?* Instead Coach Barry made Goverdhan and another thirty-something squash player run around the court juggling balls, learning the mechanics of serve, forehand and backhand. Goverdhan ran, his thighs ripping with pain, still warm and sore from his mornings practice, his head cloudy, his shoulders scrunched together mirroring his knotted brows.

At nights he dreamt of his youth. He saw himself reading a book on a second class berth under the flickering night light of a Western Railways train. *The biggest regrets are those things that we have never done.* He saw himself eating puris and *aloos* at the mid-way station. He saw himself in the exact moment when he decided that he would see America and teach himself English. He dreamt this dream many times; the train moving fast, faster, fastest, Goverdhan running, panting, running, barely managing to keep up.

Mondays were dizzy, Tuesdays and Thursdays were sore. Only the water was kinder, gentler. In three weeks he had left the wall and in six he had learnt how to float. But he stayed at four feet, afraid of five, six and seven, unable to swim in depths he could not stand firm in.

When he floated, Goverdhan meditated. He felt like a coconut in the waters of the Ganges. Was he the valuable water filled coconut his mother and grandmother coveted and haggled for with street vendors? Or was he dry? Then he remembered the other coconuts in his life. His first motel. A rundown east ender. Nalini wearing a fabulous Banarasi silk sari borrowed from an Indian neighbor. Nalini breaking a coconut each in front of the temple deity and the entry gate of the motel to propitiate the gods. More years, more coconuts, more new saris for Nalini.

But now Goverdhan worried that life might stop handing out coconuts soon. At the motel people looked at him, with his sprained neck and his unevenly tanned skin oddly. Afternoons he was often tired and involuntarily snoozed in the warm and rusting futon in his office (a remnant of his early days).

In the evenings, Arun avoided Goverdhan ever since Goverdhan had eagerly sought Arun out for their only set of tennis. Goverdhan had failed all his serves in that solitary set. Arun had tried to slow his serves in an attempt to generate some volleys, but Goverdhan was always at kissing distance of the ball never quite managing to rally more than once. As they shook hands after the set, Goverdhan ruffled Arun's hair said, "I am so happy to lose to you *beta*. Perhaps you can help me get better."

"No Dad, it's supposed to be the other way round," said Arun quietly and started walking back home.

On the other hand, uncomplicated little Varun was always busy with basketball and biking and only seen at the Yadav household during mealtimes.

Week after week, Goverdhan could feel his breath becoming progressively shallower, his body shutting down, begging for release. He felt like he was carrying a tornado inside him that would burst sometime soon. It was only a question of finding a safe place to release it. "I know what the problem is," he would tell Nalini at whispered moments at nights. "I don't have stamina... I must build my stamina."

Then one afternoon, while showing a guest her room, Goverdhan was visited by the word he had been waiting for. He felt a wave of nausea sweeping through his body. Goverdhan excused himself and ran to the nearest rest room, trying to fight the crushing sensation in his chest. His body sinking in a whirlpool, tears rolling down his brown sun burnt cheeks, staining his white stubble, he remembered a word his mother had used only sparingly. *Luupt.* Evaporated. Just like that. Luupt. Vanished like it had never existed. There is nothing anywhere. When Nalini met him at the ER seventy minutes later that was the only word he could find for her. *Sab luupt ho gaya. Everything has gone. Evaporated.*

That evening Varun saw that the table was not set. Instead Nalini was crying on it. Varun ran to her wordlessly.

"Where's Arun?" she asked wiping her tears.

"You've forgotten Ma. He's at Daniel's, its Mr. Lane's birthday; he's sleeping over after the party tonight."

"Do you boys ever remember your father's birthday?" Nalini howled.

Goverdhan was sleeping when Varun entered the room.

"It's okay Dad. I'll come back later."

"No Varun, come *beta*, sit next to me."

"Shall I press your feet Dad?" said Varun. He had never offered to do it for his father before. But from Goverdhan's stories he knew that feet-pressing was the least common denominator of devotion and filial love.

"How was school?"

"Good. We had a guest speaker today. She talked about the joys of traveling ..." and then breaking off, "Tell me about how you decided to come to America Dad."

The request filled Goverdhan with an immediate pleasure and he started....

"When I was 19 and ..." He stopped, "I've told you this story one too many times Varun." He shook his head back and forth many times, half-delirious with the Ibuprofens swimming in his guts.

Then one rainy January evening on a phone line filled with static, he heard his grandmother's voice the second time since he had landed in America. "Come beta, I have plucked the freshest rose in this town and kept her safe for you. Come now. It's getting late."

"I want to travel the world too, Dad. I want to be like...." Goverdhan thought he heard Varun and then Nalini.

"Shh. Go now Varun. Do your homework. Your father needs to rest."

When he came back that summer with Nalini he learnt the meaning of a word he would learn again and again for the coming decades of his life. Anand. Anand. *Bliss.*

The fever was still strong. His knees ached. His thighs were sore. Nalini dipped a small white cloth in a steel bowl, saturated it with water, then squeezed it dry and put it on his forehead. His wondered if he should ask Nalini to call Varun back.

"Where's Arun?" said Goverdhan.

"Try to sleep. He'll come back soon."

There is nothing in the world. It is all present at home. There is nothing in the world.

"Do you remember Nalini," he said, "when Arun was little and had just learnt to walk he'd say move, *haato*, to all the furniture that came in his way...."

Just a Photograph

When it was all done, he simply remembered the photograph. That was not where it had begun, but it could have ended there. With that photograph. He went back in his mind many times, rewind, forward, nothing, wait –or maybe something, rewind again, pause. It had nothing to do with her face. That he found it unpretty. Not ugly. Just unpretty.

It did not begin when his mother had started emailing him photographs of girls – three really – with the help of their friendly neighborhood cyber café owner. Hers was the first photograph he clicked open. His eyes had lingered on her mouth and then moved on – overcome, not wanting to unzip, download any more pictures. But mother was persistent. A week later he spoke to her over the phone and she giggled coyly into the mouthpiece and he forgot about the wave of nausea that had hit him when his face had lingered on her mouth. A few calls later he found himself in the moment when he decided to say yes - she'd been narrating a moment from her birthday party just past and in the background he could hear the diligent whirring of a robust ceiling fan. It no longer mattered that he did not like her name - conversation over, he quoted Shakespeare to himself over and over. Whenever he remembered her, he clicked open the latest photograph sent across to him. A straightforward shot of her sitting upright in the photographer's chair draped in a brown sari, no smile, no aspiration, no sorrow lines registering themselves on her face. Yet.

Quizzed by incredulous coworkers about the impending arranged marriage, "It works," he would say with a pause and flourish, "for clunkies like me," and then adjust the buckle of his belt, something he'd picked from his potbellied father, just gone, a nervous tic that looked even more misplaced on his lean frame. He was not clunky and could have found a girl on his own, but liked the idea of surrendering to a parent. They set a date soon after Diwali. It had all happened very fast. That India trip was a blur of colourful festivity - so much mithai and paan shoved down his throat! So many kurta-pyjamas gifted to him, more than he could possibly wear over the span of two weeks. A lot of it was a blur. He did, however, remember the tune of the song that had been playing in the taxi as they drove towards his friend Abhay's Delhi home for an overnight halt. A Himesh Reshamiya song he didn't like particularly. No not because of the nasal twang, he just couldn't put his finger on it.

She arrived with him; those were the days, easily on an H-4B. Very soon he became her pet project. They bought fancy clothes for him. Many clothes for her. Everyone who met her was impressed by her vivaciousness. She felt much the same way about herself. Then one night as he nibbled on her lips, she told him that she didn't like him. He laughed. *We've been married six months. Surely, you must be joking.* "Surely," she said.

Then she grew quiet and sleepy. Very. He thought it had something to do with her period. She looked so calm in sleep and when his eyes detected a slim, red rivulet of drying blood streaking down her thighs he felt vindicated. He looked at the colour of her nightgown, orange –yellow and remembered the first time he saw her – in that photograph.

She tried. He tried. She cooked. Occasionally cleaned. Cauliflower marinated in plain low fat yogurt and bananas fried in chick pea batter. He strained cups of tea for her. Strained to hear all that she did not say. Someone should have told him – *Think.... who can possess the wind*? And to her*: How long can a phlebotomist masquerade as a surgeon*? But they tried. One time she told him that his legs, she thought them too slim. Almost thin. Another time she told him about a classmate of her from the university, big-jowled, thin lipped, chain smoker. He asked her no follow up questions. They kept trying. Like a lock and key determined to fit into each other at the wrong moments. Soon Fall was upon them. Days became shorter. Darkness getting bigger.

Unable to mitigate his ordinariness he offered her what an ordinary man can offer best. Attention. Forgiveness. Trying to look at her in a way his father had never looked at his mother. He thought he was partially successful in hindsight. He suggested: *The green card will arrive shortly. You can always study? No? A Baby then?* She nodded in half-hearted agreement. To which option he did not know. At work, he looked at blinking cursors unable to write a single line of code. He felt a stab of pain when he saw his father's picture and irrationally thought that, had his father been alive this would have not happened to him. In tender moments he thought of her as a sweet mistake. And hoped that in time the sweet would overwhelm and diminish the mistake. He hoped she'd be the loyal wife. Aware of her options. Yet choosing to stay. Loyalty no longer a tribute of the subservience and ignorant.

That particular evening when he came home, he found her surrounded by a heap of cold clothes looking outside through the grilled apartment window searching for something inexplicable in the cars whizzing past the Sunnyvale temple. That took him back to the moment when he first discovered the heady rush of freedom in America, immediately after the fear that stunned him into submission.

He was at Union Square with two friends; they'd driven up north from UC San Diego, during their first long weekend. He'd been in the country all of two weeks. He had lost them. And tried to cross a road without pressing the walk button. After all he was veteran of perilous road crossing. When the echo of the honks had died down, he remembered the words of the bespectacled Chinese woman who he'd found standing right outside Macy's, "Why make it difficult when it can be simple?" she'd said so simply and without reproach and then pointed him out to the button.

That was the beginning of discoveries. On his way back to the University he discovered that he loved the Pacific Coast. And that he had in himself the appetite for several discoveries. Slowly he learnt the ways of America. That clothes folded straight out of the dryer needed no ironing. He stopped shaking his head both ways when asked a question; there were no takers for the bobble in this land. He made friends. Some only walked with him a brief distance – like the waitress who sneaked him an extra cup of hot chocolate on a cold, cold morning with a wink and did not put it on the tab. Or his erstwhile flatmate's one-year-old – the vision of his little mouse face intent on his sippy cup, his onesie half wet from earlier attempts, stayed with him for several days. Others, much like America herself, were to stay with him much longer.

And then – what joy to go back home, what relief to be back! When the airplane touched down he would pat softly on his left chest pocket of his striped gray wool jacket and know that a lot more than the paper notes with RBI Governor's signature inside his wallethad suddenly come alive. Currency notes worthless for living only moments ago, now useful, almost as miraculous as a dead man suddenly come alive. But two weeks in the once familiar and he'd long for the embracing anonymity of America, a place where he had no one and yet he longed for it. He had thought at that time that those moments were a build up to better times ahead. Now he felt such sorrow, not because those moments had passed, but because he did not drink them more fully, quench the fullness of his thirst when he had found himself in those moments. Such sorrow and anger at no one having told him, at he not having told himself. 'Enjoy this, this is a good time.' *This. Is. A. Good. Time*. He was not destitute but he felt thus. Some days he wondered what might be easier, to kill her or to kill himself. He fancied himself for Dracula and it was the thought and not the alcohol that made him giddy. Then his mother came visiting. The couple acted well for two days but a third day in their home and his mother cursed herself for trying to remedy the fact that her son had no one to call his own in America.

It was not all bad. Atleast not relentlessly so. There were days the darkness would lift. But the meteor continued its downward spiral. He meditated on the photograph often. That first photograph. She'd been wearing yellow faux leather with a false fur collar and red pearls across her long neck. The jeans a little ill-fitting. Her head and mouth tilted in opposite directions from each other. Her arched mouth a crisp ruby red. Her right leg horse-straddled around the borrowed photographer's chair. Her face was not impassive or droopy as it often was of late. No, in this first encounter with her face he had found it smiling. That was the first time he'd seen those big teeth in a petite face. It was in that moment that a wave of nausea had first hit him. When his body had warned him and he did not listen. It was not at the looking of the photograph that it could have ended. It was in what happened inside his body when he looked at that photograph that he could have saved himself. But now it was done. He was free. If you didn't count the memories.

Slowly, after many, many months he brought himself to fold clothes right after the dryer cycle buzzed. While they were still warm.

Parikrama

I am eight or maybe seven; in any case, I am old enough to be out of Dad's arms. But I am still in them. I can feel the length of my body being crushed by his forced embrace. My legs dangle and poke him alternately. I can sense that he wants to slouch, but he keeps his back straight to balance the force of the enormous crowd of men around us. There are human feet on each square inch of marbled earth of the temple hall. The crowd murmurs, their buzzing feels both tense and patient to me, long before I learn of the true meaning of either word. Dad shifts again. This crowd waits in front of a maroon curtain 20 feet away. There is no telling when this curtain will open. It feels like it never will, but it does, quite magically. The crowd bursts in spontaneous elation. "*Radhey Radhey*" there are hands all round me with palms facing the sky. Five feet ahead, separated by a gilded semi-circle, the women huddle together much like us, in a colourful sea of red, ochre, parrot green, amber. I can hear Dad's voice exhorting me forcefully, "Take the aarti Adi. Raise your palms towards the deity and bring them towards your eyes and…" The crowd is surging, pushing, pushing. There are others behind us, waiting to take our spots. We must hurry in our conversation with the Divine and make way. I can spot Amma by the enormous pearl and sapphire bangles on her wrists as she raises her arms up, before the surging crowd from the left pushes Dad and me to the exit on the right. Amma is not afraid of being crushed. She holds her spot. It feels like eternity before we see her again.

After the darshan, Amma and I walk hand in hand, circumambulating the sanctum sanctorum, our parikrama. I am wearing Corduroy trousers and a sweater with Spiderman colours.

"Amma," I ask her, she who is unusually quiet today, "Does God really live in the deity?"

She pauses in the middle of our parikrama and glances in the direction of Dad sitting languidly under the peepal tree at the far end of the hall, catching his breath and shooing away the flies. Then Amma smiles and flicks the hair that seems to perennially want to kiss her forehead. Coming down to her knees, so that we are face to face, she says conspiratorially, "You know Adi, in the brief moment that *your* eyes meet those of the deity's, the formless takes form. Just for that brief moment, Adi and only for you."

"Only for me Amma?"

"Yes, darling, only for you."

I look for my parents everywhere. In pens, pencils, in the phantoms that dance on car windscreens. Once every day, around 7:30 PM, I go and sit in their room for half an hour. I eat my dinner with them. Except for that half hour, I rarely enter this second bedroom whose presence mandates my teaching an extra class each semester. Some Saturdays, Julie comes early and dusts the room while I make us dinner. A few weeks ago she started looking through the pictures. She has now added that to her routine: dust, spray clean with cleaning agent like Windex, look through one album. She wears her hair long and down; it falls liberally over the carpet. The first few weeks I would vacuum these strands as I vacuumed the rest of the apartment. Now I let these auburn streaks lie in the absent minded vacancy of the carpet to remind me that I am not lonely anymore. That come the weekend, Julie will drive from Santa Monica to be with me. I remember the first day I moved into this apartment complex a little over two years ago. It was two months after Amma; my original one-bedroom had filled quickly. "Are you sure you want to do this? We could put away a few things in storage?" asks Matt, my best friend who is helping me move in or out, or whatever one might call that. In that moment I imagine what it would be like to smash Matt's face, to have his teeth and blood on the floor. *My parents are not going to live in storage.* I shake my head; say quietly "I got it man. I'll just get a bigger apartment in a few months."

This particular Saturday, Julie is late. She is paying the price for speaking her mind. But a 14-hour weekend round trip is hardly the stuff that will bring her to her knees. She calls me from her cell.

"I hope you have dinner ready. I could eat a dinosaur."

"How was class?"

"Great! Everyone loves me *there,*" she says wryly.

Like me. I want to say. But I don't. There is something about these cell phone conversations that make me recall the first time I met Julie, eighteen months ago. She sat next to me in a faculty meeting, a once-student prodigy and now veteran of the adjunct world. Me, a newbie, grateful to have a classroom to go to every morning. She didn't sit beside me for very long. Ever so often, someone would bring her to her feet. When she finally sat down, I said to her, "It's a good thing you like the world."

"And how would *you* know *that*?" she snapped, flicking her bangs away from her eyes.

Faculty meeting over, Julie followed me out, excusing herself from a conversation. She stopped me in the hallway, came up to me and looking at me right in the eye and said, "You might as well join me for coffee. That way I'll get an equal chance of figuring out if you like the world too."

And after that she sat beside me on all meetings for the next twelve months. Till the department threw her out.

Even though Julie is late she must do her routine cleaning triad. Over dinner, she pushes an album with some photographs sticking out in front of me. I shake my head, the spaghetti suddenly feeling very dry and nauseating. "Yes, you can." She says firmly. It's an album of my first year in this world with one additional photograph I have never seen before.

It's a photograph of Amma and Dad, looking like children themselves. The picture is in colour but has a faint sepia tint to it. Amma is wearing a fuchsia sari with large geometrical patterns. It's flying in crazy directions in the wind but modesty isn't the foremost on her mind. She is laughing with her hands clasped to her ears, while Dad is standing on a bended knee a few feet away with his fists up in the air. The Taj waits patiently for them in the background. I want to send this photograph to a competition with the caption "Happiness".

After Julie leaves, I phone Deb Mama, rousing him in the middle of the night. Deb Mama is my mother's brother, my only surviving kin from the first circle of my family. He is five years Amma's senior. Since the day Julie picked up his phone in my apartment, his voice carries an unusual buoyancy whenever he speaks to me.

"I thought Amma and Dad didn't have a honeymoon." *Our lives were the moment, Adi. Our lives were the moment.*

"They didn't," said Deb Mama.

"So what's this..."

"It's probably from the time when they ran away to Agra and Fatehpur Sikri for two days right after the wedding so that I could work on your grandfather." He chuckled.

"And then..."

"Your Nanaji was like a coconut. A hard shell with a liquid inside. Asmi came back; that was enough, he forgave Joey for stealing his daughter's heart. The week after that trip they flew to New York via Paris."

The airport is full of little shrubs of families. They stand in groups, sipping lattes and mochas and eating pasty donuts and sugar-laced pastries, appearing untouched by the longing that permeates your life once reality becomes the past. These are people whose sartorial preferencesAmma would have giggled about with good-natured disdain, "Is good taste a rare genetic attribute?" she would ask exasperatedly, while Dad would tease her about being a snob. "Asmi, everyone is not friends with rich people who are friends with even richer people who live to be seated in the front row of ..." Quick to take a slight, Amma would cut him off, "Sweetie *that* is totally uncalled for! I knew how to keep the colours fresh even when all I had to call my own was a small suitcase of saris."

These tall, thin, short, fat people with black, brown hair are people I envy because I am homeless on Thanksgiving and heartbroken in summer. These are people I envy because they have parents while mine are gone without having witnessed my graduate degree, my first job, my first serious girlfriend, my fiancée, my unborn children.

Julie brings us both coffee and sits quietly by my side. She is wearing the Julie Uniform, a navy blue jeans with a cotton office shirt. She wears no jewelry save for two barely visible diamond studs in her ears.

Julie is determined not to look glamorous. It's bad enough being pretty. Her bangs are her only feminine indulgence. Julie plants a chaste kiss on my cheek as I am about to enter security. "Hey, smart guy, don't grind your teeth while you sleeping, ok." I squeeze her by the waist towards me. I wave to her as the line moves forward. Julie refuses to leave even as I motion her to go. Suddenly she is calling out.

"I know what I am giving you for a wedding gift. A night guard." Typical of Julie to give priceless gifts casually. Some of the bystanders look shocked, other suppress a knowing smile. I crinkle my face just a little.

"Thank you. In my defense it's hard to be awake when you are sleeping. Amma left something for you in the locker. The keys are in the usual place."

She nods, blows me a kiss. I can't tell if she's crying. Very unlikely.

They make me remove everything. Shoes, socks, a forgotten pencil stub. I am okay. My bag beeps beeps. They open it. "What is this?"

"They are dancing bells, gunghroos," I explain to them. *Take a little bit of Amma with you,* Julie had said. I picked up the nosiest item. The security guard shakes them near her ear. They speak just like only they can. *Chaan chaan, chaan chaan.* She takes one little sound bead in her hand and looks up at me.

"Go ahead," I say with resignation.

Peeling it would be futile. After ten minutes of waiting, someone resourcefully produces a tiny hammer. They break the bead with the hammer. It comes clean. They break another bead, then another.

"How about we add this bag to your check-in luggage?" She is a little ashamed by now.

"I don't have any."

"Well, then this will have to become one," she says.

I open my mouth to say something. "Let him go Martha," an older officer interjects.

"He's fine. I can tell."

And then to me, "Have a wonderful trip sir."

A thousand knots live in my feet. I sit near the window, not my usual aisle, with a little pillow and an undersized blanket; I feel like a bear cub huddling in a cave. It reminds of the last time I was in a cave. It was two days before my 16th birthday, and at the end of what would eventually become our last trip to India as a family. Amma had wanted to seek the goddess Vaishno Devi's blessings for many years. Finally, Dad decided to indulge her.

We'd trekked 12 miles of hilly terrain, battled cold, cold showers, low oxygen and high altitude nausea to reach the stone cave. The culmination involved a pathway each one entered on his or her own. Just like birth and death, no two people could walk together in that passageway. As usual, Amma went in first.

"Dad, why are we doing this if we don't believe in god?" I snapped.

"Ah, but we believe in your mother," Dad said briskly. "After you Adi."

Amma was in love with the mystery of God. Dad was in love with the mystery of Amma.

People die like they live. Amma liked to plan, refine, clean up her mess. Therefore, somewhere in Santa Clara in a locker under my name lies an enormous red velvet covered jewelry box with all of my Amma's once-dear baubles. During her first round of chemo Amma took off whatever little was left on her. Like her wedding ring. "Tell her," she said softly as she shut that box after caressing its skin, "Tell her I love her very much," while I stand at the corner of my parents bed, mute, unable to say, to scream out to Amma, *No don't say that. You will meet everyone in my life. That will not happen. That will not happen*. Because I know now as I did then, that *it* does happen.

On the other hand, Dad, although stubborn, was the freewheeling guy. Our typical weekend, almost till I went to high school was something like this. Dad goes out to run an errand. Calls us two hours later, "I have three tickets for the concert at the Oakland Arena this evening. You have thirty minutes."

"What is all this sweetie? Always rush, rush. Why can't we plan things a little?" Amma running down the stairs to accost Dad as we hear the garage door, with a just opened bottle of mascara in one hand and a chiffon scarf in the other. Her lips are burgundy; her eyes are bright.

It was the first break of my freshman year. Dad had bought three tickets for my favorite musical.

"How about we see it one last time?" he had asked. I shook my head.

"My bones hurt from the plane journey, Dad. Why don't you take Ms. Perennially Single Barbara, while I grab a few winks and comb my study?"

Barbara was Amma's trusted and loyal junior curator at the Museum. Amma had groomed her for years to take over after she would retire. The former Barbara did, the latter Amma didn't.

Dad didn't argue about my decision not to join them. He no longer argued about anything since I had been accepted to MIT. In the middle of the second act Dad turned to Amma with a sharp look of pain, his hand of his chest and said, "Asmi I can't breathe..." Something about Dad's tone made Amma go crazy, she and Barbara took Dad by the hand towards the exit. Barbara was holding Dad by the hand, while Amma followed a few steps behind, searching her purse furiously for her cell phone. Two steps before the exit, Dad turns, moans for what seems like eternity to Amma and falls at her feet. His fingers having faltered in their attempt to caress Amma's face one final time. On all nights before I close my eyes, I can see Amma screaming, screaming, screaming. I can see the world of the concert, a whirl, with my father's prostrate body and my mother hunched on his lifeless form, its half-pulsating heart.

My calculations are all messed up. I don't know if it's okay to call London time but I call anyway. Deb Mama picks up on the first ring.

"How's Hong Kong?" he asks.

"Nobody is smiling at me Deb Mama. I miss America's canned kindness." We laugh.

"I wish you'd have gone this route to Delhi *bacha,*" he sighs.

"It's faster this way," I say and then because I have a sneaking suspicion that he knows that I no longer care about anything being fast or slow. "I'll halt in London on my way back Deb Mama and we'll go to Paris together."

"We will," he says "For sure."

Throughout the funeral ceremonies, Amma holds my hand and kept whispering, "Don't be so sorry, baby. It's not your fault. It's not." She decides to keep the house. More for me than herself, I think. She refuses to let me transfer closer to home. Everything is still meticulous but not quite. Amma stops colouring her hair, the whites in her hair appear more and more brazen each time I come visit. She still listens attentively but her spirited engagement with life is gone. Amma's eyes are always searching, searching. Waiting for Dad to return from the concert. Waiting, waiting. Everything is a paler, muted version of itself. The house feels naked too. Not bleak, only bare. That vacancy in Amma's eyes does not go away with anything the world can offer her, raises, awards, positions of power. For the next half decade, she continues to circle this relentless fire of grief and longing, pouring everything the world gives her in this fire of oblation. But the Thanksgiving of the year I started graduate school, I saw a clarity in Amma's eyes that frightened me. I knew immediately that something was wrong, that our lives would soon become a blur fading in and out of hospital rooms. That bit by bit Amma's body would become so inhospitable, separation from it would no longer be a concern. I am gasping for air in the past. I bring myself to the present for some air. The airhostess sees me shivering and brings me another blanket. The shivers don't stop.

India accepts very easily. I have come to steal a little of her acceptance. Arun Uncle is waiting patiently for me at the airport. At three a.m. in the morning. Amma and Dad's black book has taught me a new version of *Open Sesame*. I can pick any number in my parents' enormous black book and all I need to do is to dial the phone numbers with the appropriate international code and say, "I am Joey and Asmita's son" and people will flock to airports, train stations and busy intersections. Then they will buy me train tickets, open their homes to me and feed me at odd hours.

"Thank you Uncle," I say as I bend to touch Arun Uncle's feet.

He chokes and lifts me half way in the process, "What thank you, *beta*, it's been so many years." It has. Arun Uncle last saw me almost two decades ago in the season of Spiderman sweaters. Amma and Arun Uncle both sprung from the same modest surroundings. Amma met Dad and the Fulbright Scholarship. Arun Uncle, I suspect, met most of the things he was expected to meet.

The Goel home is a modest Delhi Development Authority apartment with whitewashed walls. The kitchen is its smallest and dingiest aspect. Each piece of furniture seems to have a functional utility except for the glass cabinet above the recessed arch in the wall that holds their petite television set. In the soft night light, I see that the glass cabinet is a menagerie of fading photo frames, porcelain babies, glass animals, shellac snuff boxes, enameled pencil stands and more. Kiran Aunty is up waiting for me too.

"Will you eat something?" she asks warmly, wiping her diabetic perspiration from the loose folds of her sari. I am not hungry. But no one has offered me anything in a long, long time. I say yes and Kiran Aunty gets to work. The Goels are empty nesters save for their four-year-old granddaughter Mridula.

"She's sleeping right now," Kiran Aunty says apologetically as she sets a plate of yellow lentil dal, a sabzi of carrots and peas with roti and a sweet in front of me.

"Sonia and her husband are away for a six-month short-term assignment to Australia and with both of them so busy with work, they decided that the best place for little Mridula was with us. For a little while at least," Arun Uncle explains.

I spoon a little bit of Kiran Aunty's dal in my mouth and am stunned at how sharply I want to howl. It's as if Amma has cooked it. It's soft but each grain still has character, with a hint of tang and cilantro and a generous garnish, *tadka* of ghee, asafoetida and mustard seeds. I exhale. Exhale. Arun Uncle insists I sleep for a few hours. I retire to a small room with yellowing walls and handmade quilts and sleep uneasily. My heart remembers Amma and Dad as a distillation of their purest qualities. But in my dreams I sometimes see the trailers of movies that I am determined not to see. Dad's monotonous silences. Amma's feeble attempts at conversation around the dinner table. The door slamming between Dad and me that started around middle school. I awake drenched in sweat with Mridula standing in front me, asking me who I am.

It's Monday but Arun Uncle has taken the day off for me. We spend the morning playing with Mridula and figuring out my itinerary to Agra. In the afternoon, over endless cups of tea they show me old photographs of Amma and Deb Mama and Arun Uncle. Cracking walnuts in the backyard of their old homes. Photographed in celebration of their rare acquisition of new clothes on Diwali. The last one has Dad in them. He stands sandwiched between Arun Uncle and Deb Mama. It's an unusual picture on two accounts; all three of them have a head full of hair. Dad's hair is blonder than I can remember; Deb Mama and Arun Uncle's are jet black.

Arun Uncle asks me about the last two decades. I pause to reflect. How do you tell someone the story of your childhood? I close my eyes. I see swirling tea cups in Disneyworld, bruising bike races with Matt, and then inevitably, Dad on the floor of the concert hall, Amma's lap cradling his head. I try to resurrect, in broken sentences, my childhood for Arun Uncle and Kiran Aunty. "I was always a good student, I loved... love reading," I start in Hindi, but I speak in halting, formal sentences. "Like Asmi," Arun Uncle nods proudly. He switches to English, sanctioning a parallel move on my part. When I am comfortable, Arun Uncle switches back to Hindi and for the rest of the trip we stay put in our zones. He enquires in Hindi, I respond in English and vice versa. I tell them I am shy. "Like your father," Arun Uncle purses his lips in mock disapproval. I tell them about racing my once best friend on lazy afternoons, of falling and bleeding, but never really hurting. I tell them how each bruise made Dad prouder and Amma more anxious, of sandwiches and shakes waiting diligently for young boy's ravenous appetite. I tell them about Amma dying. I tell them how she becomes more and more beautiful as her hemoglobin levels dropped, as her voice became hoarse and her illness took deeper roots. More beautiful and graceful than when we dressed to go to concerts at Carnegie Hall.

"Do you have pictures?" Arun Uncle asks.

"Just a couple. Amma was vain; she'd snatch my camera whenever I'd pull it out of its cover in our hospital room. You have your father's habit of taking pictures of me whenever I am worst dressed, she'd say and wave me away."

Suddenly we all fall silent. I shoot a glance outside the window; it's foggy outside and our room is dimly lit. This is my first afternoon without sun in India. "She didn't want me to grieve too much about fading away,

I guess," I try to lighten the atmosphere with a feeble half-smile. I tell them that we played checkers, chutes or ladders or some other game almost each and every day in the final six months. "Medication didn't do much to alter the fact that she was sore loser," I say. Arun Uncle shakes his head. I tell them how Amma walked the long stretch of our family room a week before she died, just to trash all her painkillers. *I want to be fully awake at the most important moment of my life, Adi.* Kiran Aunty gets up to make some more tea. Her face is wet. This is all the silent crying she can do and must now retreat to the safety of her kitchen for privacy.

By late afternoon Mridula is tired. She runs around the coffee table a few times while eating lunch and then suddenly in the middle of the meal of rotis and okra that she is being finger fed, she decides she can take no more, flops down on the sofa and fall asleep in something like 20 seconds. Kiran Aunty clicks her tongue and crinkles her forehead. "She always wears herself out before eating her lunch and sleeps on an empty stomach," She says dejectedly. I sit in faded green sofa chair with white floral crochet cloth napkins on its arms, watching Mridula intently. Mridula sleeps with ease. Her heavy maroon sweater and her prone posture make her breathing almost imperceptible. I wonder what it is about breath that once it leaves, a much loved body suddenly becomes such a fearsome thing.

As dusk approaches, Arun Uncle reduces the volume of the TV and asks me quietly, "What did she say at the end Adi?"

I pause. No one has asked me that question. Till now.

"I am so sorry Adi Baba," Amma says using an endearment she hasn't used for me since childhood. She raises her cold, clammy fingers to me and I caress them in my palm which looks giant by contrast. I want to hug Amma, but I know her frail chest bones cannot take the weight of my skull. "I am so sorry to leave. But someone will come in my stead Adi. Remember that always."

I snap back in the moment. "She said I am going to meet your father Adi,"

From the kitchen I can hear some more sobbing. Another pause.

"So where is she?"

I look at Arun Uncle blankly for a second.

"The Ganga?" he volunteers.

"The Pacific," I say and just then Mridula wakes up from her late afternoon nap.

I do not tell Arun Uncle that the will commanded me to take Amma's ashes to the Ganga. But Amma changed her mind about Dad and he found his way to his beloved Pacific. I do not tell Arun Uncle how Amma had driven herself and me, one violently rainy afternoon to the Golden Gate. How we parked and walked and walked till we reached an isolated spot on the pedestrian walkway, Amma shivering, drenched wearing Dad's enormous jacket. When we were convinced that no one was watching us, Amma exposed a small copper urn from inside her jacket. These I scattered, perched on the walkway, in the beckoning, frothy, blue waters of the Pacific. I did that a second time around sans Amma, wearing Dad's jacket. I figured what Amma thought right for Dad applied to her as well.

I want to give angel faced Mridula something, but I have nothing to give her. I give her Amma's gunghroos. She flings them across the room and then has her grandmother drape them over her feet.

"A dance for us *choti* Mridula?" asks Kiran Aunty and Mridula complies demonstrating moves copied from the latest Hindi blockbusters. Amma's gunghroos chorus to Mridula's effervescent giggles, *chaan chaan chaan.* She keeps dancing till there is music. We tire on her behalf and eventually turn off the music player, so that she will stop. Mridula finishes her act with a daring twirl around the sharp edged centre table. Then she drops her head in my lap and as I caress her hair, she kisses me on my cheek and smiles just a little shyly.

We have overslept and barely made it in time for my train to Agra. The Taj Express.

"I hope you will not mind the second class," Arun Uncle says for the umpteenth time as he helps me settle in, "The first class seats were all booked."

"Don't worry Arun Uncle! Everything looks great." The train window shutters are draped in morning mist. A co-passenger helps me raise them up as the train pulls away from the platform. Arun Uncle stands there waving at me, like a perpetual motion machine. As the train pulls away from the station I see him wipe his eyes. I wonder what lives or dies inside me that refuses to let me melt.

I share the compartment with a young family. Man, woman, child, grandmother. The boy seems as old as Mridula and sleeps curled in his grandmother's lap while the mother and father adjust their luggage. A few minutes into our journey he wakes; his mother busies herself pouring him some Bournvita from a steel thermos. She assiduously avoids eye contact with me, but I can feel her gaze on me each time I look outside the window. The first time, I glance back sharply and find her dusting some imaginary particles off the pleats of her showy crimson sari. The second time I am somehow overwhelmed by compassion.

Grandma sings to the boy.

There is a little thief in the bylanes of my heart

He peeks and sticks his tongue out

Today is the day I am going to catch him

This ditty ends in tickles.

I close my eyes and try to picture the incandescent Taj. I can only manage to conjure up Amma and Dad from the picture that brought me all this way. The young family readies itself for breakfast. The man steps away for a while, to the toilets I presume. I continue looking out of the window, the tracks criss-cross each other, meeting, leaving, staying. The aroma of the food from the berth across is intoxicating. I am suddenly angry at the malfunctioning alarm clock that has deprived me of Kiran Aunty's parathas.

The man returns, the water dripping from his face onto his hand towel and the floor of the compartment. It's now my turn to step away. I notice as I walk away that the younger woman wears a lipstick that matches the color of the henna on her hair and that she is nudging her husband for a private moment of conversation. I walk towards the compartment door. It is open and I am the sole recipient of its generous breeze. The train comes to a halt. Peddlers sell tea, samosas, pakoras, pethas, you name it. I am pleasantly surprised to see that many of them look fresh and untouched by flies. Perhaps it is the winter.

A peddler sings the same song Suman Aunty sang at the memorial hosted for Amma by her museum folks.

This fist

So tight, so full of life

Destined to slip,

Like sand in wind flight

The train restarts. I continue gazing at the boisterousness of life around me. Lush countryside, cows, women carrying firewood, unwashed children with matted hair playing gaily in the fields.

I feel a tap on my shoulder. It's my reticent

neighbor. He hands me a paper plate with some food on it, half smiles and is gone. I keep looking at that plate for longer than I can recollect. Then I realize that in those sloppily cut potatoes, once crispy but now soggy puris and a few teardrops, the formless has taken form. Only for me.

Agony Aunt

Three hours after her flight took off from Singapore, Rohini realized that she had not once worried about the things that she had thought she would worry about - *Would Nayan behave well? Would she feel suffocated cooped up in a tiny chair seat for 24 hours? Would Pradip arrive on time at the San Francisco airport? What would it feel like to see him after 8 months?* Instead, an entirely new set of concerns had presented itself – *What would it mean to live as a foreigner for 365 days a year? Would it get harder to remember Ma and Baba's faces if she saw them only once a year?* Already their visages seemed paler and ghostlike in her memory. *Would she be so lucky to find a friend like Snehlata again in …what was it called …in yes, Sunnyvale. How would Nayan take the change? What would it mean to speak English all the time? What would it mean to lose a home, a language, a memory?* As Rohini tightened her grip on her 16 month-old son Nayan, sleeping unfazed by the air turbulence that had rattled all passengers and brought the seat belt sign on, she felt engulfed by an overwhelming sense of inevitability. Adjusting the flimsy blanket on both their frames, Rohini wiped involuntary tears, unable to distinguish if they were tears of joy, relief or fear. What she could sense however, was that these tears were unlike any of the tears she had shed in the previous months and that this would not be the only time she would shed them.

"Are you alright Ma'am?" the air hostess sought her out after she'd spied Rohini rub her eyes repeatedly. "Would you like some water?" she offered. Rohini nodded and gratefully gulped the water down. Still nothing seemed to wash away the taut and bitter taste that constricted her mouth and throat, much like the permanent beetle nut stains that were splattered on the walls of the narrow lane that led to her parents' house in Kanpur.

Pradip was waiting for Rohini at the Arrival Lounge of the San Francisco International airport. He gave her a squeeze around the shoulders and quickly took charge of Nayan and the luggage cart. Even though they had left the limiting presence of a joint family thousands of miles away, yet they carried their public selves into their private time with each other. "Any more?" asked Pradip as he adjusted the luggage in the trunk of their second hand navy blue Honda Civic. Rohini shook her head, wiping the perspiration off her forehead from the loose end of her sari with one hand and holding on to Nayan with the other. They drove wordlessly from the airport to their apartment complex. In Sunnyvale, the Joshis' had a one-bedroom apartment with a small balcony on the side. With its bare walls smelling faintly of a mixture of mustard seeds and cigarette smoke and its sloppily made twin mattress, Rohini's bedroom reminded her of the bachelor digs her brother had shared with friends near the Lucknow University years ago. Pradip made Rohini some tea and pointed her out to some take out in the refrigerator. He then gave her a tour of the small apartment and a detailed explanation on how to use its various appliances – the heater, the microwave, the dishwasher, the oven and finally the gas stove with electric coils.

"How can I make rotis on these electric coils?" Rohini was immediately nervous.

"Don't worry? They'll come out fine," reassured Pradip.

Then Pradip asked her to peek into the bathroom. It was a small rectangular space, six feet by two feet, packed with a yellowed sink, a toilet seat and an ivory colored bathtub.

"Where's the drain?" asked Rohini her eyes searching for a hole in the floor.

"There's only one drain here, in the bath tub," said Pradip.

"And where do I wash the clothes?" her head on her hand and her forehead now a web of lines.

"For that we'll need to use a communal coin laundry across the street," said Pradip.

Rohini knitted her brows and asked Pradip to help her make some milk for Nayan.

The following day, Rohini and Nayan's first morning in America, Rohini dutifully got up and made some breakfast for Pradip. Not the elaborate *parathas,* ghee fried potato pancakes that Pradip liked in India, but a simple semolina snack, needing only two iterations, one for the burner to be turned on and two for the spiced semolina to be stirred constantly before allowing its latent heat to cool with water. Rohini had hoped that Pradip would be grateful for home cooked food after months of Taco Bell and hole-in-the-wall retuarant meals. Perhaps this would bring her a little peck on the forehead, maybe even a squeeze around the shoulders.

"No need to bother with such things here," said Pradip when he looked at the hastily cleared up table set up with breakfast – semolina *upma,* bananas, and spiced tea.

"Milk and cereal will do fine as well," he added. Suddenly the back ache that Rohini had filed away to push through breakfast returned. She felt her body stiffen and tighten and her breath become shallow and sparse. Maybe some sleep would help, she thought. It didn't.

For the rest of the week, as days turned into nights and sorrow into self pity, Rohini slowly unpacked her goodie and blessing filled suitcases - snacks, sweets and fritters, clothes, *puja* items and a copy of the latest *Indian Womanhood* that she would never throw away. Two weeks later, the Joshis' bought something for the first time as a family – a stroller. For $80 (in very good condition) off Craigslist. The idea of some other child with his or her soiled diapers, having used the stroller made Rohini cringe, but financial prudence won over motherly hesitation.

In America, Rohini felt like a newlywed again. Uneasy, paralysed, wanting desperately to belong. Thank God there was Nayan. Needing to be fed, bathed and played with Nayan. In the afternoons, Rohini would sit next to a perpetually sleepy Nayan and stroke his hair and cry silent tears. Sometimes, she would look outside her tiny apartment balcony. Often, she would dose off herself and dream uneasy dreams; dreams in which Rohini saw herself opening her apartment door one morning to find her maid Purna standing outside; Purna's blood shot eyes and sallow complexion appearing strangely comforting and almost beautiful. "*How did you get here*?" Rohini would ask Purna incredulously. "*I followed you elder sister, so that I could help you with household tasks. The houses are so different in this country. You need help.*" Rohini would wake up in a cold sweat after all her Purna dreams, and it would take many, many cups of tea to restore a semblance of warmth.

"Go to the park, make friends with some Indian kids and their moms," Pradip would repeat parrot-like each evening. The park was Pradip's answer to the colour slowly draining from Rohini's face, the extra salt in the vegetables at dinner and the snappyness that Nayan had to endure from his mother every now and then. Every other weekend Pradip would drive Rohini and Nayan to the nearest outlet mall and treat them to a salad buffet. Rohini would stare at her plate full of cold chick peas, carrots, lettuce, corn and beetroot silently wondering if her feelings of invisibility stemmed from the fact that everything in America, from its potion sizes to Malls to its freeways, was huge.

*

The cars whizzed past Rohini merging into a shadowy background. With a restless and tearful Nayan tugging at the corners of her long tunic, Rohini was suddenly regretful of her rash decision to walk to the neighborhood drug store. A decision prompted by Pradip's careless remark in the morning – 'It'll get better'; a remark that made her want to smash her tea mug engraved with the words Californiawas *So Expensive, I Could Only Afford Half a Cup* at the door after Pradip. But she quickly controlled the impulse because she knew she would *have to* clean up the mess herself. As she saw him walk towards their car from the balcony, Rohini wanted to run after Pradip, shake him and ask him over and over - *What will get better?* This forced house arrest, the sterility of these bare walls, this incessant cooking and scrubbing, the unfamiliarity of the climate, a life where the only uninvited sound is that of a smoke alarm that goes off at regular intervals? *What* will get better?

It was this rage that drove Rohini to take the two-mile walk to the drugstore, on an empty stomach with crumpled 20 dollar bills stuffed in the baggy pockets of her oversized olive sweater, pushing Nayan in his stroller. At the check-out counter, she checked out a gallon of whole fat milk and a thin composite notebook and hesitantly replied "yes, yes" to the store clerk's

"Did you find everything okay?" Even though she did not joke and chit-chat with the store clerk the way the Indian-looking woman in grey pants and maroon turtleneck ahead of her did, Rohini decided that if each day were accompanied by such small triumphs she could live in this country after all. Outside the drugstore, however, in no time this triumph turned into panic, as Rohini realized that she had never paid attention on how to retrace her path. Pradip had driven them to this store for four months, but it was so difficult to navigate this sea of sameness, so different from the familiar comfort of the narrow g*allis* of her childhood, where each by-lane was distinct and populated with acquaintances to help you out if you lost your way. *A hollow victory this trudge has turned out to be,* thought Rohini, as she held Nayan's fingers in the left clammy hand, while awkwardly maneuvering the gallon of milk and the stroller with her right hand. Just then she saw the woman who'd been ahead of her in line, reverse her silver gray Volvo and pull up next to her.

"Hi, I am Aditri. Can I help you?" the lady in the turtleneck enquired.

Aditri looked like one of those models splashed in the feature articles of *IndianWomanhood* with titles like 'Take charge of your life' and 'The 21st Century woman'. Aditri, with her kohl-lined eyes and neatly sprayed hair, looked like she belonged behind the steering wheel.

"I think I am a little lost," Rohini replied hesitantly, fighting back the tears.

"Don't worry. Hop in – we'll figure out where you need to go," replied Aditri brightly. While Rohini did not remember exact directions, she had managed to memorize her address and the important landmarks leading to her home. Aditri punched-in all these details into her GPS and they were on their way. Rohini was immensely grateful as they drove up to her apartment complex.

"There we are, all in one piece. Without a child seat *and* a traffic ticket," Aditri half-smiled as she let Rohini out.

"Are you Indian?" asked Rohini, surprised at the urgency of her voice.

"Well, yes," replied Aditri wearily.

"Would you like to come up for a cup of tea?" asked Rohini, hoping against hope that this woman would say yes.

"Another time. I live not too far away from your complex. Perhaps I could stop by some time after work," replied Aditri.

A week later, on a similarly cold and cloudy afternoon, the door bell rang. Rohini was putting away her clean laundry while keeping a shrieking Nayan under control and away from the remaining pile in the basket ("The shame of taking your dirty clothes in a basket in public view to wash them and then bringing them back in the 'same' soiled basket!" she had complained to Pradip the first time). Rohini's heart sank. Who could it be? Nobody ever knocked on the door here. Two weeks ago a kindly old turbaned gentleman from Ludhiana had been shot dead during the late night shift at the neighborhood 7 Eleven. Rohini took the phone in her hand and pressed 9-1-1 on the dial pad just as Pradip had directed her to do in the face of any emergency. Peering through the key hole, she saw it was Aditri.

"Oh Hello! It's you!" said Rohini nervously as she opened the door.

"Yes – it's me, Aditri," Aditri gushed breathily. Aditri looked at the phone in Rohini's hand and asked, "Did I come at a wrong time?"

Half-embarrassed, half-flustered, Rohini could only mumble, "No No. I am fine. Would you like some tea? I was just finishing my laundry for the week. It seems interminable."

"Yes," said Aditri. "Yes, to both of them, the tea and the fact that laundry never ends."

Tea, cookies and samosas later, Rohini decided that Aditri was the nicest person she had met in America.

"How do you like it here?" asked Aditri.

It was a simple question, asked with a commonplace casualness, but it reduced Rohini to tears. She shook all over as she got up to keep the tea cups in the sink. Nayan took a temporary reprive from his attempts at trying to grab the salt and pepper shakers from the dining table.

"I know... it's hard," said Aditri quietly and rubbed her French manicured fingers up and down the bony arch of Rohini's back.

"And you?"

"I came to this country when I was 18 – a long time ago," Aditri winked. "It's easy now. I don't remember anything else." Soon Rohini had composed herself again and was moving her fingers gently through Nayan's tousled hair while Aditri kicked off her heels and sat at the edge of the sofa.

"You look really smart," complimented Rohini. "Is your dress from Talbot's?"

"Smart and Talbot's?" Aditri burst out laughing.

Rohini smiled too, though she wasn't sure why Talbot's should not be considered smart.

"I must get going now. I have a meeting in the area," said Aditri glancing at her watch. At the door she paused and ruffled Nayan hair and pulled his cheeks, "Remind me what's his name again?"

"Nayan, meaning eyes…. I thought we would have a girl and had picked out Naayantara, the star of my eyes, for her," smiled Rohini.

"Nayan works very well too! Doesn't it, little man?" teased Aditri. Nayan hid shyly behind his mother.

"Will you come again?" asked Rohini just as Aditri was about to leave.

"Yes, I will," she said.

In the evening Rohini animatedly recalled her day to Pradip, "Imagine! Who has the time to be so nice here? Are you listening?" Pradip snorted, and changed into his nightclothes before spreading himself out on the sofa with his laptop, and was quickly consumed by its alternate universe.

True to her promise, Aditri came to meet Rohini again. And again. And she never came empty handed; each visit Aditri brought something to help Rohini understand America a little better- a copy of the latest news magazine, a coupon for a clothing store, the phone number of a driving instructor. Soon life fell into a routine. Mornings were for cooking, cleaning and napping and the occasional driving lesson. Late afternoons, early evenings were for Aditri to take off early from work and drive Rohini out to malls and coffee shops with Nayan safe in his new car seat (Craigslist again). They looked quite an odd pair – Aditri in her power wardrobe, boots, diamonds and coloured hair, and Rohini in her loose tunics and ill-fitting and slightly short jeans that made her look like a delicate piece of okra. On weekends, the husbands would join in as well. Aditri and Anil were unlike any couple Rohini and Pradip had met. While Pradip and Rohini saved assiduously for a future that often dwarfed their present, Aditri and Anil seemed to live in the moment.

"So do you have any family in the U.S.?" asked Pradip.

"Nope! Thankfully not," replied Anil, taking a swig from his Martini glass.

On Rohini's first birthday in Sunnyvale, Aditri signed her up for a class to learn to make bath fizzies and tub treats. At Aditri's insistence, Pradip was persuaded to watch Nayan for an entire Saturday while Aditri treated Rohini to a pedicure followed by a manicure, before dropping her off at her bath fizzies class. "Be very careful," said the instructor, "too much Citric acid and you will have a rather pungent bath bomb, too much Witch Hazel and the bomb will crumble before you can pack it together. Find the right balance for the warmth of your palm!"

That night, Rohini wrapped her rainbow coloured bath bombs in pink satin bag and tucked them away in a small drawer in her bedroom. Then she said a small prayer thanking God for bringing Aditri into her life.

There was something wonderful and intimidating about Aditri. Rohini was not sure which attribute she found more overpowering. Rohini loved the effortless way in which Aditri's english fell out of her, the way she opened her mouth in the shape of an 'O' to say Hello, the meticulous care she invested in herself, and her spunky and go-getter attitude. Aditri made Rohini feel that she had truly come to America. With Rohini, perhaps Aditri felt that she too had come home once again, to India, however fleeting that might be.

Six months into their friendship, Aditri threw a bombshell.

"I've taken a transfer to New York," she drawled

"Why would you do that?" asked Rohini perturbed. "I thought that you were very well settled here."

"Because the Big Apple is where the action is... I don't want to be a petty cog in the wheel for the rest of my life. I've been taking it a bit easy in the last few months and I need to get my act together."

"And what about Anil?"

"He is a little upset right now. But he'll come around and join me there soon enough."

"Come on, Aditri, you can build a good career here too," said Rohini.

"Well, how would you know? You never really had to face problems like mine," Aditri shot back. Rohini bit her tongue and swallowed hard. Yes, she wouldn't know. Then Aditri Dutta Roy simply packed her bags and left.

Two Thursdays after Aditri left, Rohini got her driver's license. "It's a big thing. I'm so proud of you. We'll celebrate tonight!" Pradip said excitedly when he dropped Rohini and Nayan back home. The cordless' rings greeted Rohini as she stepped in. It was Aditri.

"Oh Aditri! I have missed you so so much. I am really glad you called. I got my driver's license today."

"Hmm, that's nice, Rohini," Aditri replied weakly.

"Rohini..." Aditri was crying, muffled at first then stronger an instant later.

"What's wrong, Aditri? What happened?" Rohini whispered in the phone hoping that her soft voice would soothe Aditri's nerves. Aditri continued sobbing.

"Look Aditri, it's not like you are right there and I could give you a hug and make it okay. Aditri you must take care, you must hold yourself together, you should not fall apart like this. Tell me what happened."

"I am not sure if I did the right thing by moving here. I am having so many problems at work and I think Anil is having an affair behind my back as well."

"Come on Aditri, you trust Anil more than that, don't you? And I am sure work will get better."

"I don't know," replied Aditri.

Two hours later Nayan had gone to sleep watching Barney on the living room sofa while Rohini put her cordless back in its cradle to recharge. This phone conversation with Aditri had been the longest of her life so far and she felt slightly unnerved by this shaky side of Aditri's temperament. As Rohini rubbed her ear lobes to lighten their deep red colour, she hoped that she had cheered Aditri enough to succeed in her presentation the following day. Rohini had never felt so useful in her life.

The following Monday was an uncommon one. The Joshi's had plenty of food left over from the weekend get-together they had hosted for Pradip's co-workers. Nayan was bathed and fed and put to sleep without too much fuss. Rohini's feet ached from the weekend's cooking and cleaning. Perhaps today would be the day to free the bath bombs from their satin womb. Rohini let the water slowly fill the tub, its rhythmic sound reverberating in their tiny bathroom and suffusing her with a sense of ease. Then she slowly slipped out of her cotton nightgown and dropped the bath bomb into the tub. Just then, the cordless phone called out to Rohini again. She hurriedly put her night gown back on and ran to the phone.

Aditri's voice was broken, softer and flatter than Rohini had remembered it from the last time on the phone.

"Aditri, what happened?"

"Anil... he's not taking my calls, and I'm having such a bad time at work," Aditri's concerns had only become more magnified.

An hour later, Rohini switched off the cordless; the bath water had become cold and "unsoakable". The bath bomb had lost its form. The day was done. Rohini put the phone down and thought of how her conversations with Aditri had changed since she had gone to New York. Before, they would talk about books, makeup, hobbies and colours. Now it was just Aditri with her woes and Rohini with her reassurance.

A week later Rohini had just put the breakfast on the table when the phone rang. Pradip picked it up this time.

"Rohini will call you in some time, Aditri."

In between the toast and semolina *upma, Pradip* asked her. "What's going on?"

"Aditri's having adjustment problems and Anil doesn't seem too supportive," Rohini spoke quietly as she added butter to Pradip's toast. Pradip noticed the hint of darkness on her face when she spoke of Aditri.

"Do we see another Aunty Naureen on the horizon?" Pradip tried to lighten the mood a little. Aunty Naureen was *Indian Womanhood's* famous Agony Aunt. Aunty Naureen had answers for everything from the serious to the mundane. Many times the answers were those that you had been avoiding yourself, but she vocalized them for you. Rohini wondered what Aunty Naureen would say to her problem. The last two times that she had spoken to Aditri, she had been so drained that fixing a simple meal had seemed a Herculean task. For each positive suggestion that Rohini could offer, Aditri found ten others to discard them. Should she call Aditri and risk the loss of another day? Should she? As she debated her decision, Rohini glanced at the floral shirt on top of her clothes pile – another gift from Aditri. Everything about Rohini's life in America seemed to have Aditri's unmistakable stamp on it. There was no escaping her presence. Rohini picked up the cordless and pressed redial. When they signed off, Aditri said, "Thank you so much Rohini. You're the most patient listener I know."

Mother used to call Rohini a "chatterbox", *bhaiya* called her "talking train", Mrs. Jacob, her botany professor in college, had called her "overly inquisitive". Rohini wondered at what point she, of all people, became a "patient listener". Perhaps it was somewhere between being a whiz kid's wife and a woman looking forward to seeing human faces on her supermarket trips.

"What did you do today? Did you read something?" asked Pradip in the evening. Rohini shook her head and busied herself with getting the dough ready for the rotis.

The next weekend was a long one, so they decided to visit Sita Aunty in Toronto. When they got back, the answering machine was blinking with twenty-seven messages, all Aditri. "Rohini, call back man!" The last message was standoffish and snappish.

"I think you need to ease off from her," said Pradip.

"She is my only friend, Pradip. She needs me. Besides, this is my chance to be there for her like she was for me."

Rohini grabbed the newspaper and dumped the clothes in the laundry basket while dialing Aditri's office number. "Hello. Can I..."

"Yes, Rohini, it's me."

"How are you, Aditri?"

"I am fine. How are you? Hope you enjoyed Canada and are enjoying your new car," Aditri said condescendingly.

"Ohh," Rohini felt inexplicably defensive. "The last time we spoke I had meant to tell you, but..." her voice trailed.

"It's alright. I have my sources too!" Aditri laughed.

"Look, Rohini, I have a meeting coming up in two hours, let's talk later." With that Aditri signed off, leaving Rohini to ponder the snub for an entire week.

"Let Anil and Aditri figure out their lives themselves. Why do you meddle?" Pradip said another night.

"I can't leave her now!" Rohini said, half shrieking, before collapsing into a heap.

Pradip glared at her. "Life is not a Hindi movie. Try to be less melodramatic," He said quietly.

"Yes, yes, I am melodramatic. And if you didn't think the way you do, maybe I would never have felt the need to be melodramatic. Do you know how hard it is to start the day with a sense of possibility and then to see it eroding as the day passes by. Do you know how hard it is to see the walls of your house cave in as dusk approaches? To have a mind and to do nothing with it? To have no one to talk to? To keep doing housework all the time? You don't know, Pradip, because when you get up in the morning you have a place to go to and people to see."

"Rohini, please, Nayan will wake up." Pradip reached forward to touch her.

"Let him, someday he has to. I crave for attention and because you never gave it to me, I seek it from Aditri. I am so disappointed," Rohini flinched from Pradip's touch and stormed off to lock herself up in the bathroom. Pradip followed her, knocking on the door softly.

"Rohini, Rohini, I am sorry, let's try to find some solution. Rohini…."

"There is no solution to this deafening silence," Rohini whispered hoarsely from the other side of the bathroom door.

"There is, there is, Rohini. Maybe you can learn something, go back to school now that Nayan is starting pre-school. Rohini, please listen to me...."

A few days later –

"Where have you been?!" Aditri bellowed irritatedly into the phone.

"Oh, Nothing much.... I went to pick an application form for a Certificate in Apparel design at the community college."

"I don't know why you do all these things, Rohini. If I had a husband like Pradip, I wouldn't have done a thing!" said Aditri.

Rohini clenched her palms and then unclenched them. Then she picked up the bottle of pickles lying on the table.

"Things are tough for me too, Aditri. Pradip and I have been having some communication problems."

"Well then, honey," Aditri drooled "You just wait for your green card and make your way out."

Rohini was aghast. This was a friend? A friend whose best counsel to a tired embittered soul was to make her way out from marriage? No one ever made out from marriage - she and Pradip were together in it, not just for this birth, but also for the next seven births. (And more, as Pradip had often told her). Rohini decided to change the topic.

"How are things with Anil?"

"He's finally got a job here and is going to move to New York soon. I was wrong about his having an affair. It turns out that he was afraid that I would hook up with someone who would satisfy me more!" Aditri laughed triumphantly. Rohini felt like someone was shaking a metal can full of glass pebbles close to her ear.

"That's nice," said Rohini

"After that we plan to start a family. I don't know how easy that will be – we've been trying off and on for a year and I am already 34. God, do you know how lucky you are, Rohini? You already have a child, and a boy to boot," Aditri barely made any attempt to conceal her envy. Suddenly Rohini felt a tightening sensation in her chest.

Tears stung her eyes as she summoned up the will to answer Aditri. "Having children is not like graduating from school or things you do before a certain age. Things happen to people at different points in their life. One must be content with what one has. Ma had me when she was 17; I had Nayan when I was 25. It is not fair to compare."

"Still ...you are one hell of a lucky woman," Aditri said before hanging up.

Rohini felt like her tongue was stuck on a slab of ice straight out of the freezer. Her mind was whirring…. *"Bitch!"* *"Where's Nayan"*, *"After all that I did for her*….

Nayan was playing with plastic yellow duckies in the bath tub when Rohini spied in on him. She took him by the hand to the kitchen and made him stand near the gas stove. Then she took a pinch of salt and red pepper in her fist and moved her fist in circles seven times around Nayan's head just as she had seen her mother do to protect her children against the evil eye. Rohini then dropped the mixture on a hot pan, even though she knew that the smell of the burnt spices would throw her and her child into a coughing fit.

That evening Rohini made Pradip buy her a caller ID machine. A few days later when the cordless phone announced ADITRI DUTTA ROY, Rohini picked up Nayan and stepped out of her house, shutting the door and the phone's loud wails behind her.

Big Didi*

*Hindi: Elder Sister.

As far back as I can remember I have wanted a *didi*, a big *didi*. My husband, Rajat, tells me that calling a *didi*, a '*big*' *didi* is redundant. As if I don't already know. But then, all of us have the right to christen our yens as we deem fit. At six I exhibited a proclivity towards making myself snug in the laps of female college-going cousins. At ten I asked my parents why they didn't have someone before me, convinced that it had been an aberration for me to come in first, before my baby brother, and before that unborn older sister. My parents' responses were not particularly satisfactory; my mother blushed and my father roared so loud that I can still hear the echo of his laughter.

I have subconsciously sought an answer to that question ever since – and I am now twenty-nine years old, the last five of which have been spent in Sacramento, Palo Alto, and Sunnyvale. As I inch gradually southwards, I hope that this southward motion will eventually propel me back to the south

163

of India, Bangalore ('That's eastward motion' Rajat again). But until then I must be content here.

No, content is the wrong word. I am actually reasonably happy. I will not say 'very' happy because *dadi* says that one should never use superlatives to describe any situation, whether sorrowful or happy. Finding a commonplace adjective to describe sorrow reduces its intensity and averts potential escalation, while just the opposite might happen if you flaunted your happiness. But then, you are not reading this to have me share my childhood sermons. So I'll quickly rewind to March, almost a year ago. My birthday falls on the 2nd of March and this humanly designed watershed annually induces in me a self-pity masquerading as introspection. Last March was not particularly different, except in intensity.

While Rajat attributed *my Down syndrome* to a flu virus that had overstayed its welcome, easily bribing me to take a day off from work in exchange for 'an evening full of rapture', I knew better; for I had witnessed my angst build up sneakily much like that faint and moldy yellowish growth found on the baseboards of even the tidiest bathrooms.

My immigrant years had enveloped me in a bubble of bereavement – the erosion of family ties, the labor of daily life, and the lack of spontaneity in social interactions had all taken their toll on me. When I contrasted my once heady days, full of a sense of possibility, to my present circumstance brimming with superficial rituals of gift–giving and tab keeping of 'who-called-us-for-dinner-and now-its-our-turn', it made me thirst for something deeper, something more authentic. I felt short-changed and spent – often noting that while I would walk more than the extra mile for most of my friends, they always seemed to call in sick when it was their turn.

"You *know* that's not true," Rajat would remonstrate, "and you never really ask for help."

"I don't like to ask. If they are *like-family*, they *should* know," I would shoot back.

"Birthday girl, don't you dare drive!" Rajat hollered from the garage while I nodded listlessly from our living room futon. Forbidden to drive, and commanded to rest, there wasn't much to do; I showered, ate, tried to read and then most naturally cascaded into slumber. A while later I was roused by the shrill cry of my Panasonic cordless.

It was my neighbor Jalaja. *How about a cup of tea?* I knew instinctively why I had been bestowed this honor. '*Her elder sister must be out of town*' a tiny voice inside me whispered tartly. That voice was right;   baby-sitting-gift-giving-tea-making-elder-sis was out for some R&R. Mostly I had blinded myself to this fact, but today was my day. I refused, kept the phone down and promptly burst in tears. The evening brought Rajat home a bit early from work; his gift for me -- a delicate pair of teardrop earrings in a petite red satin box. Unfortunately, he did not have any box to imprison my tears, which meant that our candlelight, Pinot Grigio, gnocchi and tiramisu had to wait until my wounds were cleaned.

"Wish I could buy a *big didi* at Walmart!" I sobbed into Rajat's lungs.

"Why don't you try *craigslist*?" he retorted. At that we burst into a fit of spontaneous laughter but unwittingly Rajat Shourie had given me the answer to all my *big didi* problems.

Rajat has always been partly-amused, partly-sympathetic to my desire to have an elder sister.

"Look, Mohini, you do have Jayant. Unlike yours truly." Easy for him to say. Perhaps, not so easy ... and yes, I do have Jayant, my surprise gift a day before my ninth birthday. For years I listened to Ma and Papa say, "Be kind to him, Mohini. You are his *didi,* he is just a baby." Whenever Jayant would hit me (which was often), I would get scolded. His birthday would be the official day we celebrated our birthdays, while the second of March would be compensated with what at that time seemed like afterthought gifts and absentminded kisses. Afflicted with the *Sunday night syndrome*, Jayant would remember deadlines with barely enough time to come out alive. Each year I filled in new blanks - help Jayant memorize a chapter, give a speech, write an essay, design a scale model, or prepare a questionnaire. I often wanted to be halfhearted with my help; which would lead to mediocre results and my subsequent freedom. But I didn't want Jayant to fail or be laughed at, so I plotted my own enslavement and stayed encased in that cage. It was not as if in return for doing these thankless jobs Jayant would honor me with his confidences. I was his pride. Yes, if there was an equation he couldn't solve... **his** *didi* could! But talk? Nah!

Then at age twenty-three something happened which relieved me of all my Jayant-related vicarious tensions. Rajat Shourie, only child of Justice Shourie came to India from Harvard; and Papa labored to convince me that my PhD *must* be temporarily kept aside in favor of his acquiring such a brilliant son-in-law. The first time I met Rajat I couldn't believe my good luck...this man had come to marry me? There had to be something wrong with him. It was too good to be true.

But hey, I am digressing, looping one story into another. Unlike Rajat, always focused. A year later, after weeks of festivities and *seven pheras* (or *seven rounds* as my *phirang* hubby refers to them) around the sacred fire, I found myself in America. Full-of-sale-bargains America. Loneliness-inducing America. Lesson-teaching America. At SFO the customs official asked me the meaning of my name. Mohini. Or Mo-HINNY as everyone at work calls me. It means 'bewitching'. "*Tum to moh se bhari hui ho, beta.*" ("You are full of love, my child.") That was my *dadi's* interpretation of my name. Yes, I tried to give as much as I could. But increasingly I found myself resenting it. I give. I love. But who loved me? Rajat? My parents? Jayant? Rajat loved spreadsheets and overtime. My parents loved the sound of my voice powered by AT&T. And Jayant? Well... whatever.

Two days after my birthday, my body cracking under post flu duress, I accidentally dropped a mug full of chai on the kitchen pergo, sobbed uncontrollably for two hours and then fearlessly placed this ad in the community section of *Craigslist*.

Wanted A Big Didi...

Who will love me unconditionally. Make Aloo Paratha and Garam chai when I am low. Buy me dresses when my birthday hovers. Pampers me when I have a baby. And what will I do for you didi? Listen to you. Love you. And I know that will be enough, because you will be 'my didi'.

Reply to: waitingfordidi@yahoo.com

When I saw the posting online, I felt the tightness of a well-written paper in my belly. Now there was nothing to do but wait. And wait. For a while I didn't get any responses and soon the fears that my hysterical bouts of crying had temporarily plugged returned. And *then...* there was Spam - porn sites, antidepressants, anonymous inquiries ('*what exactly is a didi*?'), to people trying to hit on me. Unknowingly I had become like those unhappy people on talk shows; people I had watched with shamed engrossment, relieved to know that *that* particular agony had not come my way.

And then it happened. To borrow Amy Grant's words... *The lights came on in the House of Love.* After two weeks of despair, sadness and disenchantment, when I was just about to take off my posting, I got the following email.

Dear Possible Sis,

I chanced upon your email while scanning the community pages of Craigslist and my heart welled up on reading it. I have a strong instinct that I am older to you and I want to be your didi. How about meeting at SF MOMA next Friday, at 11:00 am? I will be wearing a crimson scarf. More when we meet.

Possible didi

I promptly dashed a reply to yours@yahoo.com, taking care to reserve calling her *didi* till the D-day.

Thank you for responding! Friday it is - I'll be either in the café or on the 5th floor. I'll be wearing a maroon skirt with beige stripes and a brown turtleneck. Besides the crimson scarf, how else could I identify you?

Possible Sis.

Her reply...

You will know me when you see me... on the 5th of April.

I was ecstatic. My good luck had overturned the laws of nature. I debated internally for eight hours whether or not to share this news with my pragmatic hubby, eventually succumbing to Yudhistra's curse* on women. Rajat was stunned. It seemed to me that he was better equipped in dealing with bad news rather than good. He had taken the news of my previous 'spammer' emails rather well after having forgiven my 'childlike' transgression. But now he went ballistic.

'How can you be sure it is a woman? How can you be sure she/he is not going to whisk you away somewhere? Na na... And how can you meet her on a working day!'

"I am taking the day off from work. I need to unwind anyway." He frowned. But I eluded his guilt/get-some-sense-in-your-head trap. Finally, he gave in. "Just be careful. Keep the cell phone handy. Call 911 first, then me. It will take me almost an hour to get there. Do you want me to come with you?" The last question he retracted hastily after seeing the scowl on my face.

The rest of the week went by in a blur. I was hardly myself, sometimes anxious, sometimes delirious, *always* speculating about *her*. On the big day, as we stepped out of the house I opened my mailbox to collect yesterday's forgotten mail, (a habit that irks Rajat, impatient to transport our Saab into the carpool) and quickly stuffed a sky blue envelope with a familiar handwriting in my purse before running to the passenger seat.

On the Caltrain I opened the envelope. It was a 'Belated Happy Birthday' card and Jayant had tried to rev it up by making a pyramid with the letters M-O-H-I-N-I, pairing each letter with an adjective: M for Marvelous, O for my One and Only DIDI, for H for Happy, I for Incredible, N for Naughty and I for Interesting. I felt a stab of guilt for being angry with him for not sending me a card on my birthday and sent him some trans-Pacific mental hugs to atone for it. (Trust me... they work. The receiver feels loved.)

From the Caltrain station I took a cab to the SF MOMA as I did not want to be late and the kind cabbie got me there on time. I was at the MOMA ten minutes to eleven - I quickly grabbed a *mocha* and took a nice seat in the open-air section of the museum café. From that vantage point I had a bird's eye view of all those who came in. As I waited for *didi* designate (DD), my mind was furiously churning those all too familiar questions. What was she like? Was she of Indian origin? A vegetarian or a non-vegetarian? Did she enjoy Seinfeld, Shahrukh Khan and Saffron *Kheer*?

As I sat there, my nerves on Orange Alert, no one escaped my furious scrutiny. Suddenly I saw a lady with her head covered in a scarf. My racing heart could have easily broken all Olympic records.... only that scarf wasn't crimson. '*Maybe crimson is at the cleaners; Blue's nice too.*'

I got up quickly to make sure that my skirt pattern was in full view, but she quickly averted my gaze and went inside. I was sort of relieved. The head-covered-scarf–lady would probably be having beef at home. (Not that we ate any kind of meat at all!) Then I wondered if DD was a good cook? (Food is a major ingredient of affection, isn't it?) What if... she was not a Hindu (which would have been a very distinct possibility)... how would I introduce her to my family? What would they think? After fifteen minutes of stranger gazing, in a brief moment of awareness, I realized that I had harbored inside my heart, a world full of prejudice, some insidious, some innocuous, and mostly inconsequential but prejudices nevertheless. Struck hard by this epiphany, I made a feeble attempt to confront each one of my prejudices. Jane, Farida, Young and Dylan. I took their names aloud and reassured myself that my choices in friends had already broken artificial barriers. My guilt temporarily assuaged I thought 'Come on, Mohini, it's okay if DD is all this and more. What do you need after all, but someone who loves you?'

Fifteen minutes turned to thirty and my mouth was now dry from the mocha. What had happened? Why hadn't she reached on time? My anxiety was getting the better of me and I went inside and converted my e-ticket having decided to wait for her at the 5th floor.

I had been to the MOMA before and therefore was more eager to see the new addition; the legacy of Phyllis Wattis, exhibited on the fifth floor. For the most part I didn't understand it. Maybe I should have paid more attention. But it's hard when you're sizing up each new entrant in the room with one eye and looking at an artwork with another.

At 12:30 P.M. I made one last attempt to push my anxiety to the background and decided to take a browse through the remaining paintings. On my way out I was struck by a red oil on canvas, vast and expansive and with a small yellow oval in between, the two colours separated by a tiny but deep boundary. The red was so vibrant and charming; it took my breath away and pushed me into the present moment with renewed vigor. Just then, I heard some clatter behind me. I spotted two little girls, one blonde and the other auburn, sitting on the floor, their drawing books open, busy recreating the same rapture that had just enlivened me up. The auburn seemed to have stolen a crayon from the blonde's box and held on to it protectively, while the blonde continued screaming "Give me mine back!" in her tiny urgent voice. Hearing these shrieks, a figure emerged from behind the shade screen placed at the center of the hall and hurried to the girls, her dirty-blonde hair offsetting her aquiline features. Now the dirty blonde kneeled and gently moved the girls apart, placing her hands on their tiny frames. Her eyes penetrating the auburn, she said, "Come on sweetie, give that back. Be nice to Rose."

"Why?" The auburn replied, unsure of what tone to acquire.

"Because she is your sister," She replied gently and held them both close.

I blinked and turned and I don't know how but my tote fell from my hands and my contacts seem to well up unnecessarily. Frantically my eyes searched, *Restroom, Restroom.* It's a good thing museums encourage introspection. It's a good thing we don't look at people while we are looking at paintings.

In the restroom I looked at my watch. It was 1:00 PM. Ten minutes later I found myself in the museum store and another fifteen later, I was walking out of MOMA and towards the Caltrain Depot. The sky was overcast and clouds roamed like benevolent autocrats. Just as I started walking away from the museum towards the Yerba Buena Center, I heard a faint voice enquire behind me, "Did you by any chance happen to see a lady wearing a maroon skirt and a brown turtleneck head out?" My heart skipped a beat. Could that have been her? *'Of course, it has to be*!' ... a tiny voice inside my head screamed. *'Don't you want to see her...?'* and that voice became louder and more aghast while I kept walking, faster at first and then more steadily.

I am sure she must have been lovely. Like all my other friends... all of whom, I had chosen. I had gone to MOMA to meet my Big Didi but I ended up meeting her little sister for the first time. I met myself like I never had the chance before. It was 2:30 P.M. by the time I reached the Fourth and King Station. The drizzle had become a steady downpour by now; I clutched my tote hard and found myself a bench to sit. Inside my tote was a small mug that I had bought for Jayant from the museum store. As I sat on the bench I realized that I was wet. I was happy to be wet. I was happy to be who I was. *Didiless*. But loved nevertheless.

Hindi Glossary.

Roti – round flat bread to be eaten with lentils or vegetables.

Puja items: prayer items

Galli: Narrow by lane (English derivative from Hindi spelled as gully).

Naayantara: Star Eyes

Upma : South Indian semolina dish often served as a breakfast snack.

Bhaiya – BrotherChachi: Aunt

Ladoo: an Indian dessert.

Behen: Sister

Kota: City in Rajasthan famous for among other things, its lovely cotton saris.

Haan: Yes

Dadi: Paternal grandmother.

chupi rustom: Chuppa Rustom literally means "Secret Rustom". Usually a bearer of some potent, secret talent.

Amrica: America

Bhai Saab: Brother Sir – address of respect.

Aaarre: Sound of exclamation.

Seva: service

Bahu: daughter-in-law

Gobi Mutter: Vegetable dish made of cauliflower and peas

Rasgullas: Sweet cottage cheese dumplings

Banj: Childless woman

Nani: maternal grandmother

Godh Bharai: Hindu Baby Shower. Literally, it means filling the mother's lap with abundance. In the seventh month of the pregnancy the mother to be is dressed in bridal finery and lavished with gifts and blessings by family and friends.

Banarasi saris: Banaras is one of the leading silk sari producing centers of India. It is known for its heavy gold-silver brocade saris.

Desi: A term loosely applied to all things Indian/ South Asian.

Beta: child in Hindi.

Parikrama: circumambulation

In Appreciation.

I would like to extend my appreciation to the following organizations and universities: the Santa Clara County Library, KQED FM, India Currents and SAJA.

My continuing thanks to my excellent team at Leadstart Publishing: Malini Nair, Uzair Thakur, Tanzeel Saiyed, Shynu Koshy, Chandravadan Ramchandra Shiroorkar, Rajesh Bale.

My thanks to our cousin Ashok Bohra (Anil/ Aneel) for his encouragement of my writing and his nurturing support. And finally my thanks to Mummy and Nikhil for being so wonderful with everything.

May all stories find affectionate readers.

Made in the USA
Las Vegas, NV
17 January 2024

84500186R00104